W   Broome, H. B.
                Gunfighters

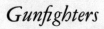

Gunfighters

also by H. B. Broome

THE MEANEST MAN IN WEST TEXAS

Gunfighters

H. B. BROOME

DOUBLEDAY & COMPANY, INC.

GARDEN CITY, NEW YORK

1987

All of the characters in this book
are fictitious, and any resemblance
to actual persons, living or dead,
is purely coincidental.

W

Library of Congress Cataloging-in-Publication Data

Broome, H. B.
Gunfighters.

I. Title.
PS3552.R6598G8   1987   813'.54   86-19864
ISBN: 0-385-23516-X

For Christie, Clay, Paul, Andrew, and Matthew

Acknowledgments

Table and data in Chapter 7 concerning Montana range economics in the mid-1880s taken from *The Works of Hubert Howe Bancroft*, Volume XXXI, pages 736 and 737, published in 1890 by The History Company, Publishers, San Francisco, California.

References in Chapter 15 to the Cheyenne war chief Roman Nose and his death at the Battle of the Arikaree (a river also spelled Arickaree), or the Battle of Beecher's Island, are matters of historic record.

Indians, pages 343 and 345, by William Brandon, published in 1985 by American Heritage, New York, distributed by Houghton Mifflin Company, Boston.

Plains Indian Raiders, page 190, by Wilbur Sturtevant Nye, published in 1968 by the University of Oklahoma Press, Norman, Oklahoma. (Credit given in this book to the Smithsonian Institution, Bureau of American Ethnology.)

Gunfighters

CHAPTER ONE

The people in the saloon seemed frozen, their mouths open. I
didn't really give a damn what they thought.

"Great God a'mighty," Joe Case bellowed from where he
stood behind the bar.

I turned toward him, and his startled gaze fixed on me—
looking first at the Colt .45 in my left hand and then at the
brimming glass in my right. He whispered, "You didn't spill a
drop."

It was dead quiet in the Concho Street Saloon. The poker
players who had jumped to their feet stood now with five or six
cowboys and three of the girls. They moved to both sides, form-
ing a kind of aisle. I passed through them on my way to the
swinging doors, which I shoved open so as to step outside. My
boot heels made hollow noises on the creaking wood plank
sidewalk as I walked, and my spurs jingled a little with every
step. Two men stepped off into the street to get out of my way.
None of us said anything, but I suppose they knew that I'd shot
another man. The old sickness welled up. I can't stand it when
folks act scared of me.

A horse made a fluttery, low, nickering sound and stuck his
head over a hitching rail at me. Five minutes later I found
myself still scratching his head and rubbing his soft nose. It gave
me time to collect myself before I moved on.

Ben Jordan, our sheriff now, but up until recently the U.S.
Marshal for our part of West Texas, sat at his desk. He looked
older than his sixty-six years, and his hair and mustache had
turned white as snow. His face was brown and leathery and had
cracks and wrinkles in it like a dried-out creek bed.

"Been waiting for you," he said. "I already heard about it."
He rose and stepped to the small stove behind his desk where
he poured two cups of coffee from an old blue enameled pot.
Dark metal showed through at the places where it had chipped.
"Lewis Westbrook had closed his store and stopped by Joe
Case's place for a drink just as it happened. He told me he'd no
sooner walked in when all hell broke loose."

"Where's Lewis now?"

"Gone to fetch Doc Starret, though from what he says, it's a
waste of time." The sheriff sat down, cradling the thick white
coffee cup in both hands, and grunted from the effort as he
leaned back and put both boots upon his scarred desk. "Was it a
fair fight, Tom?"

"No."

Ben Jordan's eyes narrowed. He waited for me to speak, but
when I didn't he drank some coffee. "Lewis said someone tried
to backshoot you from a dark booth."

The sheriff rubbed his mustache dry as best he could on his
sleeve, then stood up. He put on his hat, fastened his gun belt,
and fixed his eyes on me. "Might be best if you wait for me here,
Tom. Whoever it was may have a backup man."

He stood there, examining me, then he asked, "How many
does this make?"

I knew what he meant. "Twenty-one, Ben. This is the twenty-
first man I've killed."

"There's no end to it in sight," he said. "Every fast gun in the
West wants to be known as the man who finally shot down Tom
English."

Things looked better in the morning. They usually do. I had a
breakfast of eggs, venison sausage, biscuits, and coffee in the
friendly, warm cafe that George Henry built last year next door
to the Taylor Hotel. To my mind it's the best place of its kind in
Santa Rita, or for that matter anywhere else in West Texas.
When I paid the bill I saw my reflection in the mirror behind
the counter. I saw a serious-looking man of twenty-eight, face

shaded by the brim of a sweaty old Stetson hat, with pale blue eyes looking kind of out of place in a weathered face as brown as any Mexican's. I looked as though nothing out of the ordinary had happened the night before. Only the surface showed, for inside my nerves stretched out as tight as piano wires.

I stopped by the bank where Max Hall looked flustered at first, and then tried to smooth things over with his usual good-old-boy line of talk. As a rule this sets well with the bank's customers, and it gives Max time to think.

"How's the richest rancher in Texas?" he asked.

"Broke as usual," I said. "No sensible banker would have anything to do with me."

"I'm not going to sit here while you poor-mouth," Max said. "And if you're running short, why don't you sell one of your ranches? What do you have now, three hundred and eighty thousand acres?"

I didn't comment, although five hundred ninety-six sections adds up to a little more than that.

"If you're so damn broke, why do you keep all that money in the Fort Worth National? Did you forget about that?" He sounded aggravated. If you've ever seen a rank horse lay back his ears and "sull" on you, you can picture what Max looked like.

I wished we could change the subject. When Max found out last year that I was using another bank as well as his, he like to have had a conniption fit. He groused about it every time we sat together.

Max turned in his swivel chair and nodded for me to sit down. "I saw you ride into town yesterday with a good-sized roll tied behind your saddle, and you had that big red roan on a lead rope. Going to Fort Worth?" The bitterness crept back into his voice.

"A lot farther than that. You remember Hap Cunningham from Sonora?"

Max nodded that he did, and I could see his interest in the conversation perk up. Hap was a fine rancher out a ways west of

Santa Rita. Some years before he had sold out to the Espeys, and moved to the Montana Territory.

"Hap wrote me that he's found a place where it rains or snows all year. The grass rises clear up to a horse's belly there."

Max snorted. "The growing season is just at three months, I hear."

"That may be, but Hap says he can get a stand of hay in those months that you wouldn't believe."

My old friend looked confused. "What in the *hell* are you talking about, Tom? Surely you of all people don't need more land to worry about."

"My worry is the weather," I said. "I'm tired of betting double or nothing like most of us do. We've been lucky and had some good spring rains, but you and I both know that it's only a question of time before the next drouth hits. Right now my ranches are paid for, and so is most of my livestock. But in a few years things could dry out, and then before long I might find myself real deep in debt like most ranchers, and from then on I'd be working for you, Max." I smiled at him as if I was joking, but he and I both knew I wasn't.

My excitement built, I couldn't hold it back. "Max, they still have open range in Montana, all you do is stake out your claim to it. And there are herds of wild horses according to Hap, free to be taken by the man who can do it."

Then I roughed out my idea for him. I said, "I'm planning to claim a place in a hurry. Benito's son, Santiago, and four of our boys from the Lazy E are going to bring up a string of brood mares. They'll start in four weeks, and I hope to find some grazing land before they arrive. If I have trouble doing that, we'll put the mares up at Hap's ranch while we keep looking. I'm taking Joe and Ross, my best traveling horses, and they're also what I consider our best studs. If we cull through those wild horses I was telling you about, we can surely find a number of good mares. In the course of time we ought to be able to develop a fine strain of cow ponies." I grinned at Max and said, "I like the idea of paying for livestock with sweat instead of dollars."

"Always been partial to horses, haven't you, Tom?" Max made it a statement instead of a question, and I admitted that I had. Both of us relaxed a little then, and we had a long and pleasant conversation.

I left the bank with enough money for the trip and with a cashier's check to deposit in Montana so I'd have some working capital.

Somehow the rest of the day passed rapidly. I talked to a few old friends and then went over to the livery stable to check out the horses. Joe heard me coming, and I poured out some extra oats for him. Ross reared up and began to kick the walls of his stall, and I couldn't quieten him down. He didn't like being inside a damn bit, and as horses sometimes do, he panicked. When things like that happen you want to stay clear, for a crazed fifteen-hundred-pound stallion in a close place doesn't make good company. Finally I got a rope on him and led him to the corral out back, and then he settled down as though nothing had happened. I was worried for fear he had hurt himself, but found he was fine.

My idea was to alternate riding the two horses during the trip. Even though Ross was a bit skittish, he and I were getting on well enough, and in the long weeks ahead I'd have more than enough time to work with him. Neither horse was shod, for in our country we rarely shoe horses, although naturally we trim their hooves. I wondered if they might come up lame or footsore when we reached the mountains, but I didn't figure on any problems. God knows, the Indians used horses there for hundreds of years, and they never heard of horseshoes.

I walked up the stairs to my room in the Taylor Hotel, wondering if I had packed everything I'd need. Making a mental checklist, I thought of my Winchester and extra cartridges, and dried beef jerky in my saddlebags. I didn't intend to eat any more of that jerky than I had to, for I'd be on the lookout for game as I rode. In a way the time spent traveling would be like a two-month hunt, and few things gave me more pleasure than hunting. The only thing that bothered me was the memory of Sally trying not to let me see her tears as I rode away from the ranch. I shook that off and concentrated on what lay ahead.

I suppose the excitement of this, taken together with the strain I'd felt all day as I forced myself not to think about the life I'd taken the night before in the Concho Street Saloon, dulled my awareness. I simply had no sense of danger when I stepped into the darkness of my room, leaving the door open for the moment, so as to use the small amount of light from the hall while I felt my way across the room to the chiffonier which had a kerosine lamp on it. I smelled a passing sweetness in the air which should have put me on my guard, but I was thinking of whether to saddle Joe or Ross the next morning, and was making my plans. I reached the high chest of drawers, struck a match that flared yellow, and lit the wick.

Strange that the sound that split the silence in the room like a whipcrack, a sound that made my heart leap and thud with surprise, should be the softness of a voice speaking just above a whisper: "Raise your hands, Mr. English, and turn around real slow."

I did as I was told. At first I thought I saw a man, for the person across the room from me *dressed* as a man, with a plain blue shirt and trousers. A heavy six-gun hung from a hip that swelled out, and a small hand held its grip. Then the person stepped from the shadows into the light, and I saw the pale face of a woman with her long dark hair gathered in a bun at the back of her neck. Her left hand held a brown silk purse.

"I expect you don't remember me." Her voice wasn't steady, and I could tell that she was very nervous. I saw her clearly now, and she looked familiar. Where had I seen her? A scattering of pockmarks scarred her face.

She said, "No—I didn't think so. I don't suppose you think about the corpses you leave behind you." She paused before stating, "I'm one of them. You killed me just as certainly as if you'd shot me like you did my husband, Earl." Her voice grew stronger now. "Like you did when you shot his brother, Billy, and our friend, Pete Harris. And after that . . ." She couldn't go on, for she began to sob, and tears ran down her cheeks. Fighting back her rage she brushed at her face with her right hand, smoothing away the wetness.

I lowered my arms and she stared into my eyes with a look of hatred as fierce as any I've ever seen. It looked like a shaft of coldest steel. "I talked to Judge Elder a while back. You need to know that I've thought this through with care. The judge is on his circuit and will be here in a week. He was my father's closest friend, and I asked him what would happen if you were ever to shoot a woman. Do you know what he said?"

I didn't move or speak.

She put her right hand back on the heavy Colt she wore. "Judge Elder said, 'Why, Mary, you know the answer to that as well as I do. He'd hang.'"

A swift, small rigor ran through me. No matter how a man may look on the outside, there's no one who can truly control his nerves all the time. The trick is to keep them from controlling him.

I remembered her, of course. Her name was Mary Dawson; and pictures flooded through my mind of the range war with the Dawsons and Pete Harris and their hired guns. I'd never forget the man in black who faced me on that muddy street when we had our last showdown. He was faster than I was, and the bullet he fired came close to killing me. But it didn't, and I killed him.

Accusingly she said, "You stole our ranch."

"I bought it, Mary."

Sparks came from her eyes. "So you *do* know me."

I added, "With the money I paid for your place on the Concho you folks bought a good ranch near Marfa, out past Alpine. I've always heard that is fine country."

In a distant way she said, "The land was strange to us. We never even stocked it before you'd killed our men. Then Louise, Billy's wife, and I sold out and moved to El Paso with the children. That's where we were when the smallpox epidemic hit. Now Louise is dead—her children and mine are dead."

Mary Dawson moved a little closer. "Take a good look at me." She turned her head to one side and then the other, and in the full light of the lamp I was struck by the sight of the angry red scars that seemed so terribly out of place on her soft face. "People once thought I was pretty," she said.

Her eyes grew wide. "You did these things. I thought of killing myself, and if the man I hired had shot you down last night, I would have. But I somehow knew it would come to this. There is no man alive who can stand up to you. There are a good many dead ones who have tried that, including the father of my two lost children."

Her small right hand tightened on the butt of her heavy six-gun, and strangely I found myself wondering if she even had the strength to lift it, much less fire it.

Mary Dawson's voice shook as she said, "I'm left-handed, Mr. English, and this big pistol feels clumsy in my right." She slipped her left hand inside the small brown silk purse, then raised it straight out toward me. "But I've got a two-shot derringer aimed at your heart. From three feet I can't miss. After I've killed you I'll pull out Earl's Colt and I'll hold it with both hands while I put five more bullets in you." In a very small voice she added, "The last bullet will be for me."

Before she could blink an eye, both of my .45s flashed out. She jumped backward, her arms instinctively crossing protectively before her breast, her eyes filling with horror even though she talked of wanting to die. But for the first time in my life—faced with a person bent on killing me—I hesitated.

Only seconds passed, but it seemed to be a long time. Then I reached a sudden decision and jammed my six-guns back in their scabbards.

Her left arm extended again and the purse fell away. She moved forward until she stood right before me. The small muzzle of her nickel-plated derringer wavered, for the hand that held it trembled. Then her knuckles whitened as her finger tightened on the trigger.

I watched Mary Dawson's face and saw her flinch just before the derringer spat forth a tiny streak of flame.

Then she stood, pale as a ghost, staring at my chest. I looked down and saw a deep red mass grow larger, staining my shirt. The numbing, hammer-like blow seemed to paralyze me.

She whispered, "It's true what they say—the devil really *is* inside of you." She backed away slowly as though in a trance, and our eyes locked together. Her gaze broke away and, with one quick shuddering movement, she put the derringer to her temple and it exploded.

She crumpled to the floor. I raised my eyes from her to see my old friend Jedediah Jackson, Santa Rita's only lawyer—standing at the open door—astounded by what he'd seen. He must have been there all along.

I saw the floor coming up at me, and I didn't try to catch myself. It didn't seem strange when my head hit. The boards were cool against my face. Then I knew nothing.

CHAPTER TWO

Doc Starret said a lung had been hit, and at the beginning it hurt like bloody hell. There is something particularly scary when it feels as though you might not be able to breathe, and that bothered me more than the pain. Now, four weeks later, I sat on the front porch of the house I built for Sally and tested myself by drawing in a deep breath.

Sally must have seen what I was doing, for she leaned down and put her arms around my neck. "Feeling better?" I nodded, and she said, "Well, I'll leave you and Jedediah out here in your rocking chairs—someone around this place has to work." Her smile took the sting from the words.

One of the best things about old friends is that you don't feel as though you have to entertain them. Jedediah Jackson—who is my lawyer, but aside from that is more like family than anything else—sat beside me, rocking back and forth in his creaky chair, as lost in his thoughts as I was in mine.

The pain had left, but not the dreams. I kept waking up in a cold sweat at night, for the old nightmare had returned. I stood stock-still in it, then went for my guns. My hands moved as slow as molasses, and a man I couldn't quite make out stood in a haze holding a six-gun which he had drawn, and he pointed its barrel square at me. I've had this nightmare ever since I shot Jack Malone at the age of seventeen, and the only way I've ever been able to drive it out has been to practice with my Colts until I feel I'm ready for anything that might come. I doubt if there's a man alive who has spent half the hours practicing that I have.

"That woman is too good for you," Jedediah said, breaking into my woolgathering. "It's beyond me what she sees in you."

He poured three or four fingers of sour mash bourbon in the glass he had been nursing for the last half hour, and savored it.

"I thought that was a get-well present," I complained. "You didn't tell me that you planned to drink it all yourself."

"You have no true appreciation for young women or for old whiskey," Jedediah declared in his lawyer-like way.

At that moment I heard the distant clatter of a horse's hooves and saw a burst of color breaking through the mesquite trees in the flat below the house. A minute later Rebecca burst through the light green branches and pulled up Skeeter, her fat little sorrel mare, to a show-off stop in front of the house. I sat there watching—proud as punch.

"Don't take much to amuse a kid," I said.

"Don't take much to amuse a parent," Jedediah responded dryly.

In the ten years that Sally and I have been married, a lot has happened, but the most important thing has been our daughter, Rebecca. She's our golden girl, with curly reddish brown hair lightened by the sun so it has blond streaks in it. She has large brown eyes like her mother's that are slanted just a little, and deep dimples when she laughs, which she does a lot. Needless to say, she rules the roost.

Rebecca is the only child we'll ever have. Doc Starret told Sally that she almost died in childbirth, and she should never try to bear another. As a result, Sally and I focused all our love on each other—and on this carefree, happy nine-year-old.

"You surely aren't going ahead with that fool trip, are you?" Jedediah asked. He must have been brooding about it, for the subject hadn't come up until now.

I didn't answer right away, but sat there watching Rebecca ride off toward the barn. Then I said, "By now I should have been almost halfway to Montana, and I need to ride hard when I get under way so as to have time to get situated before the weather turns cold. I hear that can happen as early as September."

"Tom," Jedediah said, "this makes no sense to me."

"Didn't you tell me that this last trouble has found its way into the newspapers?" I took this way to approach the subject that I had been avoiding. If he could understand my reasoning, I felt he would have to believe that it made a great deal of sense.

"Yes I did." Reluctantly he added, "A writer got wind of what happened and sent a story to the Fort Worth newspaper. I wouldn't be surprised if it doesn't appear in papers all over the country. The reporter quotes Joe Case, who says that he had just poured a shotglass full of whiskey for you, that you picked it up in your right hand when a man behind you shot and missed from a dark booth. Joe Case says you whirled, drew with your left hand, and killed the man before he could squeeze off a second shot. Then the story got a little heavy-handed, with the reporter writing that once again Tom English had drawn his pistol and killed a man who had his own gun leveled on him."

I felt the gooseflesh rise on my skin as he told me the particulars of the article, although I had guessed it would be along those lines. Ambitious young gunsels all over the state and maybe beyond would read it, and each one of them would more than likely daydream of stories that might be written about him if he should be the one to kill me.

The newspapers had kept track of me for years. After the terrible slaughter in Mexico, the time when I killed ten men, a book came out. Someone in the East took the newspaper stories and wrote a tale he called *The Rattlesnake Kid*, and in a subtitle, "Killer of 15 Men When Only 19 Years of Age." Later, after the range wars and the strange turns of fate which caused Jason Field to leave his ranches to me, and after Mr. Sam Clarke's and Culley Clarke's deaths when we inherited all their land, a second book came out called *Tom English, Millionaire Killer*. The thing that hurt the most was the way so many people stuck by the label they hung on me when I'd only been a teenager. In countless stories, and in the two dime novels I've mentioned, they called me "the meanest man in West Texas." That began after I took Joe Slade, who probably deserved the reputation, but I certainly didn't think I did.

No matter how many times I heard that description, it jarred me even though you'd think by now I'd be accustomed to it. If a man gets waked up every morning from Monday through Friday with a bucket of cold water thrown in his face, it don't mean he won't notice if it happens on Saturday.

I said to Jedediah, "I won't be coming back, at least not to stay."

He turned to me in confusion. "Tom, you've got an empire here. You can't walk off and leave it."

"I don't intend to. Scott Baker is able to run the ranches as well as I can. He's been working with me and all the foremen for the last few years, and I trust him absolutely." I paused a moment and then said, "Jedediah, I have good business reasons to find a spread in Montana. I spent some time with Max Hall at the bank going over them, and he agrees with me. But now with all this publicity, I've got even more pressing personal reasons to get out of here. I mean to *hide* this time. I'm going to disappear off the face of the earth."

He looked at me hard, but didn't say anything.

I said, "You've got my full power of attorney, so you and Scott Baker are to make all the decisions that can't be handled through the mail. I would expect it to take a good while for a message to go from Montana down here." Then I added, "If you need to reach me, write to Tom Germany in care of Hap Cunningham, General Delivery, in Black Horse, Montana."

"Tom Germany?"

"Yes," I answered. "I wrote Hap that I aim to raise Rebecca as the daughter of Tom Germany, rancher, a man who doesn't have to wear a six-gun."

After supper Sally and I sat on the porch where I'd been before with Jedediah. He had gone to bed early, for he meant to head out in his buggy before sunrise. He acted as if the thirty-two miles to Santa Rita was a hardship, and remembering his cranky comments about it made me smile as I poured a little bourbon into my glass.

"More whiskey?" Sally's eyes danced as she teased me. "Am I married to a drunkard?"

"Would you mind?"

"I'll take you, Tom English, any way I find you." She leaned sideways in her chair, put her hand on my face, and kissed me. I felt again as I had when I first knew her, when we'd both been shy young folks touched by the magic of something too wonderful for us to grasp.

"Germany," I reminded her.

"Oh," she said, then grinned at me. "Sally Germany. That sounds a little bit foreign, but it has a good ring to it. Besides, it's not as stuffy-sounding as English." Then she said, "It'll be good to have a new life, a new start."

She understood exactly what I needed, but then she always had. We sat together silently. After a time she said, "I'm scared to death, Tom." And I said I was too.

Rebecca kissed us good night and went to bed. Then Sally's new friend, Hester Trace, who had been careful to leave us alone, came out on the porch.

"If you two will stop spooning, I'll join you. You must remember that I'm younger than you are, and am still impressionable. I'm asking nothing more than that you behave with consideration, with decorum, in my presence." She burst into laughter.

I looked at Hester, a slender young woman with surprising green eyes and the blondest hair I'd ever seen. She spoke with a strange British accent which amused me. It was good to see her like this, acting almost as she had before her husband's death. Roy Trace had been killed seven months before. Hester told us only the barest essentials of what had happened. His horse came back, she said, head held sideways, dragging loose reins. She went out with the cowboys in their urgent search.

Hester St. Claire had come with her father, Joseph, to see his ranch. This marked her first visit to our country. The plan was for her to return with him to England, but he went back without her after she married Roy Trace, a widower, whose ranch joined her father's on the west side.

When she first arrived from England she brought a sidesaddle, the only one I'd ever seen. She rode with long trailing skirts, her right knee hooked around the upright leather that curved up on the right side of where you'd expect to see a saddle horn. She didn't seem comfortable on horseback, but I guess if I was riding that way I wouldn't either.

Six months after her marriage she wore denim pants and rode a standard western saddle through the brush, looking frantically for her missing husband. As luck would have it, she was alone when she found him. The cowboys missed her, and then came on the scene. She sat motionless on her horse before the big mesquite tree. Roy Trace had been thrown, and by some terrible trick of fate, his head had caught in the fork of the tree about eight feet off the ground. I guess it broke his neck, but his suspended body made it look as though he'd been hanged.

When I'd planned my original trip some weeks back, I'd asked Sally to invite Hester to stay with her so she'd have company while I was gone. It turned out that this had been a welcome invitation, for Hester had been without female companionship for a long time. When she reached us, she showed how deep her depression went. I had expected her to return to her family in England, but she stayed—alone in a strange land, alone in the big house where she had lived as a married woman for just over half a year.

Hester Trace told Sally once that she'd never marry again, but of course she would. I felt happy that we could be of some help to her, and it was a source of great comfort to me that Sally would have a friend with her during my absence.

Later that night, after Hester had gone to bed, I said, "I'm leaving tomorrow, Sally."

"I know. I saw Santiago put Joe and Ross in the corral this afternoon. I saw him pack your things."

"There's another matter," I added. "I've put away my six-guns. They're in the cedar chest in the attic."

A sharp glow of pleasure struck her eyes, then it gradually faded and her concern showed. "Will you be safe?"

She came to my chair and sat on my lap, holding to me tightly while I reassured her. I told her I'd have my Winchester, and that until I got well out of Texas, it wouldn't leave my side.

She held on even tighter, and we sat—each of us deep in thought.

I recalled putting neat's-foot oil on my cartridge belt and the two tie-down scabbards that hang from it by long loops. I'd had them made special after seeing that kind of rig on a gunfighter. To my mind it cuts a fraction of a second off your time if you have to draw real quick.

We make neat's-foot oil on our own place. It's a pale yellow liquid that hardens, and you get it by boiling the feet and shinbones of cattle. I kept a can of it at the barn for my saddle, and late in the afternoon I had rubbed it into the smooth leather of my holsters before sliding the two double-action Colt .45s in them. Then I wrapped them carefully in an old blue shirt.

Earlier I had cleaned the guns. I took them apart, oiled them, and put them back together. I hefted the right-hand gun, and it fit like a part of my body. Jason Field, who hired me as a bronc rider when I was no more than a kid, who more than anyone else really raised me, gave me this finely balanced weapon long ago. He had forsaken his days as a gunfighter, but he worked with me when I found myself in trouble. He knew a great deal about gun handling, and what he taught me saved my life on more than one occasion.

I put Jason Field's .45 away, and cleaned my left-hand gun, the spitting image of its twin, though it took me a long time to find it. When the hired killer I always thought of as "the man in black" broke my right arm with his bullet, I had practiced for almost a year with my left, almost frantic at the idea of being helpless with as many enemies as I had. When at last my right arm healed, I found that when I drew both guns the left fired just a fraction of a second behind the right. I remembered well the satisfaction that gave me. I worked after that on accuracy, and gradually the pattern that the bullets made in my targets became almost as tightly grouped with the left gun as the right.

I've often thought that in a gunfight one man or the other always has the edge, so there can never really be such a thing as a fair fight. Many is the time that people have called me lucky, and I suppose that's so, but I once told Ben Jordan that in my view luck is where preparation meets a challenge. Instinct and "muscle memory" had felled the man who tried to backshoot me in the Concho Street Saloon, for the left gun fired without my really thinking. There are times when there isn't time to think, and afterward it's best not to.

When I considered leaving the ranch without my Colts, without a tied-down scabbard on each leg, I felt a sudden sickness, a weakness that I tried to put out of my head. In my mind's eye I saw myself on horseback, and I thought of what I'd do in an emergency. The Winchester would be in its boot, in its saddle scabbard, with the stock on my left side. I always strap it there, with the rifle butt forward. It ties so the "boot" goes over the skirt of the saddle, under the stirrup leather, but over the fender beneath so there isn't anything to rub against the horse's side.

I have thought of strapping it to the right side, but that wouldn't do, for I'm accustomed to having my rope coiled there.

I had not figured out a fast way to reach over with my right hand and pull the Winchester clear. I had always considered myself to be a very good shot with a rifle, but that wouldn't help me if I couldn't get to it. Well, hell, I'd worry about that later. If I felt uneasy, I would balance it for a while on the swell beside the saddle horn.

It took me a long time to go to sleep, for I knew that the nightmare awaited me. When it came I reached for guns that weren't there, and I faced the muzzle of a close-in .45 feeling naked and vulnerable.

CHAPTER THREE

Lost again. "Damn, damn, damn." The sound of the labored breathing of my two horses on the steep trail drowned out the cuss words. Dark juniper and fir trees rose on both sides. I rode Joe, and Ross followed on the lead rope tied to my saddle horn. Thank the Lord I'd thought to buy a heavy, fleece-lined coat before I left Wyoming. I turned its high collar up on my neck.

Joe bunched his muscles and half bucked as he climbed while I leaned forward to help him. We'd been winding up and down and through the rough, wooded mountains for more than a week.

In the foothills I had ridden through grass so tall it rolled in waves before the wind. One night I struck camp with an old-timer named Newt Spence who told me that I'd see in Montana the richest feed that ever nourished livestock: blue grass, wheat grass, and buffalo grass. It laid a deep green carpet on the land, and even in the mountains I came upon wide valleys that to my eye looked choked with rich growth. In one of these I watered the horses in a cold stream so clear I could see the trout waving through it. Looking up I saw a mountain far away which still had snow on its peak. If I live to be a hundred, I'll never forget that sight—my first view of what Newt Spence had told me was the Continental Divide. On the other side all the rivers run to the west.

I kept an eye out for a good place to camp as the wind whistled about my ears and darkness neared. I had drifted off the main road onto one of those twisty side trails again, when suddenly I crested the rise, rounded a corner, and stopped in surprise. Down below me on the side of a long, hump-backed mountain lay what had to be Black Horse.

A cold mist began and I felt its wetness against my face as I leaned back, riding down the incline toward the town. The sounds of an axe splitting firewood drifted through the air, and in the distance a dog barked. The narrow trail joined a wider road, one with deep ruts in it, more than likely caused by what Newt Spence had called Concord mud wagons. He said they used them a lot in these parts to haul freight. It takes four horses to pull one, and they have big rear wheels and smaller front ones. The wagons sit high off the ground and are ideal, he said, for rough mountain roads and for fording streams and rivers.

I pulled up Joe's head and we stopped so I could look around and get the lay of the land. Black Horse's main street, a muddy patch between frame buildings that crowded together, ran on fairly level ground, but several twisting roads crossed it and angled up and down the mountain's side. Most of the structures in the central section were two stories high and made of logs with mud plastered between them. A few were built with rough boards, and two were made of rocks and looked a little like the way the Germans built their houses in Fredericksburg, back in Texas. Nearly all the downtown buildings had false fronts with signs on them, and a board sidewalk connected them. A shed roof hung over this to protect people from the weather. Logs lay about here and there as well as barrels and uncollected trash. I saw axes beside a new house under construction, and a heavy, curved steel foot adz, the kind used for dressing timber.

No one payed me the least attention as I threaded past the freight wagons that lined the street. Some of these were clearly the Concord type I'd heard about, but most were like you see everywhere, the ones with hoops covered with droopy, worn canvas. The sounds of a banjo came from one saloon, and a piano banged out a tune across the way from it. Miners, buffalo hunters, and a few cowboys crowded around these two places, and from the looks of these grimy men they were serious about their liquor. I didn't see a smile on a single face.

I had about given up on finding anywhere to stay when I saw a place that looked very much like a house, but which had a sign on it which said Elk Antler's Hotel. They had one room left, a little one out back on the second floor.

Behind the hotel lay a livery stable, so I put my horses there, and carried my rifle and saddlebags with me, leaving my bedroll, pack, and saddle with the old man at the stables. I explained to him when we turned Ross loose in the corral that he'd need to give him plenty of room, and to be careful, for Ross tends to get nervous around strangers. We put Joe in a nice, warm stall, and I paid extra for oats as well as hay for both horses.

The hotel had a bathtub which I could use for fifty cents, and after I had cleaned up and put on my other set of clothes, which were as clean as I had been able to get them a few days back in that cold mountain creek, I went back to my room and slept for two or three hours, dead to the world.

Later I went downstairs and ate enough steak and potatoes for two people. Feeling refreshed I stepped out into the cold night air to look things over. Although it was toward the end of June, the weather seemed, at least to me, like midwinter. A roman-nosed horse turned his tail toward the wind, and busied himself with gnawing at the wood of a hitching post, gulping air in a peculiar way as he did. Funny how a few horses can get into this bad habit. I slapped his nose to try to make him quit, but he wouldn't. Like most humans a horse will act mortally offended if you try to correct his manners. He shied back, flattened out his ears, and then began to bite at the wood again.

"If I give you five dollars, will you take that horse off my hands?"

I looked up, surprised, and saw a good-looking young cowboy grinning at me.

"No." I smiled back at him. "I could use the five dollars, but I don't believe I'd take that horse if you offered to give me fifty."

"You sound like you're from Texas," the cowboy said, walking

up closer. "I'd have guessed that from the crease of your hat."
Then he said, "My name's Thatcher Stone."

He stuck out his hand and I shook it. "Tom Germany," I said,
examining him. Thatcher Stone had friendly brown eyes,
brown hair, and a straight nose. A handsome kid, and he knew
it.

"Pleased to meet you, Mr. Germany. I'm from a place we call
Valentine, which you probably haven't heard of. It's about a
two- or three-day ride southeast of El Paso. Where do you come
from?"

I avoided the question. "Cowboyed around," I said, "here and
there. Then decided to ride up here to see Montana."

"You rode? The whole way? You ain't heard they got trains
nowadays?" He had an easy smile. The cowboy looked to be
around nineteen or twenty. He had a curious band made up of
Mexican coins around a carefully shaped black hat, and he wore
big roweled spurs that clanked as we walked down the sidewalk
and into the saloon.

I only gave him part of my reason: "The way fences are going
up a man won't be able to make a trip like that much longer.
Besides, I've always wanted just to head out and travel." My
answer seemed to satisfy him. I added, "Besides, I've got a
young horse that I couldn't get close to a train."

"Well, hell," Thatcher Stone drawled as we sat at a table, "I
know what you mean about wanting to head out to a new place.
I done about the same thing as you, but I did take a train
whenever I could. Then I made the mistake of buying that
rough-gaited horse you seen outside." He shook his head before
he said, "When I come into a town, I reckon that the eyes of
every horse trader there light up. They can spot a likely mark."
He grinned ruefully before adding, "I have always liked horses,
but damned if I'm a good judge of them."

Thatcher Stone went to the bar and returned with a bottle of
whiskey and two glasses. He wore nice-looking clothes I saw,
now that we were inside with plenty of light. His gun belt
slanted toward the right where it supported a tooled leather

scabbard. He saw the direction of my glance and he said, "This here is brand, spanking new. It's a Colt forty-four, and I bought it because it uses the same ammunition as my rifle, a model seventy-three Winchester which takes a center-fire forty-four cartridge."

We tried the whiskey and then he said, unable to conceal his curiosity, "There aren't many men out here who go around unarmed."

"No," I agreed, "there aren't."

He took another drink. "I haven't seen a lawman since I left Kansas, and from all I hear there are plenty of outlaws around."

"I expect you're right," I said. "Naturally, I carry a rifle. I like to hunt."

His eyes brightened. "Me too."

"But I don't see any sense carrying around a load of iron all the time. As far as outlaws go, I didn't run across but one man in the last week, and the only danger he presented was that he nearly talked me to death before I could get away from him."

A pretty woman wearing a very low-cut red dress walked up and stood beside our table, waiting for one of us to invite her to sit down. Thatcher and I looked at each other, not knowing what to say. Then he jumped to his feet, trying to cover his confusion, and whipped off his hat.

"My name's Georgia Wichita," the woman said, smiling just a little. "You boys look like you could use some company—besides, my feet hurt." With that, she sat down, and after standing there looking stupefied for a minute, Thatcher did too. While we stared at each other, she raised a hand and waved it at the bartender. A few minutes later he brought her a glass, and without ceremony she poured some of our whiskey in it.

"I rent out the upstairs of this saloon," she said. "I've got some pretty girls I brought all the way from Chicago to tempt you choosy cowboys. All them miners and buffalo hunters that hang out mostly across the street, they don't care what a woman looks like. If they was to wake up and find a hog in bed beside 'em, they probably wouldn't pay it any mind." She nodded her head vigorously. "That's a fact." Then her laughter rang out.

I looked across the table at her. She couldn't have been much over five feet tall, and appeared to be in her early thirties. She had a small nose, bright eyes with an impish gleam, and seemed very sure of herself. She acted right proud of her figure, and with reason. I looked over at Thatcher and he appeared to be as flustered as I was.

"Here's to good times," Georgia Wichita said, and held her glass out in front of her toward us. Then she took a strong drink and closed her eyes as it went down. She made a little face and shook her head, and finally she sighed. "The nice thing about whiskey is that it kinda rounds off the corners; after a while you forget the dirt and the boredom. It even helps you overlook rude cowboys who can't seem to say a word, and just sit there staring at you."

That broke the ice. First Thatcher spoke and then I did. We at least gave her our names and said we had just ridden in, and she allowed that wasn't news to her, and then she let us know that she was acquainted with every damn man within a hundred miles of there.

After we'd had several drinks, Thatcher excused himself and walked off to the end of the bar where a pretty young girl in a ruffled yellow dress stood by herself. We had both watched several men approach her, but she acted as though she wanted to be left alone, so they walked away. When Thatcher reached her side, he looked as if he'd lost his nerve. He turned and started back, but she must have said something, for he turned around. The next thing I knew, they were talking, and then they went off to a table in the corner. Thatcher's shyness seemed to melt away, and I saw him talking to the girl like a delighted kid. I couldn't keep from smiling. Then I glanced over and saw Georgia Wichita watching me.

"That's Emma Lake," Georgia said. "She is young and still mighty particular." Then, as though she were talking to herself, she added, "A girl has to get over that." She poured herself another whiskey, then said, "Emma's tougher than she looks, and I think she'll make it. Hell, she has to—there isn't any other choice for her that I can see." Then, as though she'd been too serious, she forced a laugh and it sounded full and round and musical. "Our job," Georgia Wichita said, "is to take some of the dullness out of life. Everybody needs a touch of excitement now and then."

She toyed with her glass, turning it this way and that, watching the light from the coal oil lamp play on it. Then she asked, "Are you planning to look for work, or are you passing through?"

"I have a friend, Hap Cunningham, who ranches somewhere north of here. He told me it's about a day's ride at this time of year. I'll spend some time with him, and then decide." I asked her if she knew him, and she did. By this time I had about run out of things to say, and I could feel her eyes upon me. I saw the quiet, amused expression of her face.

Finally I had to break the silence. "You're a mighty pretty lady. I'm surprised . . . you chose to come way out here." I'd spoken without thinking, and changed my course in mid-sentence. She understood what I meant, though.

"I was married once," she said, "but Jim Wichita thought that gave him the right to beat up on me. He tried it once too often when he decided that J. K. Cade paid me too much attention, and J.K. busted his head with an axe handle. It happened right down the street." She gestured with one hand. "Jim died—I was stuck out here with no way to support myself." She flared up. "I was alone; I didn't have a red cent. What in hell *could* I do?" she demanded. Then she softened. "I know you aren't judging me —you haven't accused me of anything. I shouldn't have spoken out like that. What happened later was really pretty simple. Buffalo Ed Schoonover, the man who owns this place—you may have heard of him, he used to be a hunter—well, he told me I could have a real job at his place instead of working part-time the way I had been. I was still pretty, men liked to be around me, they bought whiskey for me and drank a lot themselves.

Then one thing led to another." Her voice trailed off for a moment. "Anyway, the first thing you know the herds came in with the men from Texas, and things began changing around here. Ed sent me on the new train line to Chicago, and I came back with five girls; a few got married, but there is always someone like Emma Lake who shows up broke—someone who has to find a way to keep body and soul together."

She stopped. "Why am I telling you my life story?" She looked a little embarrassed.

I can promise that *I* was embarrassed. I never really talked much to a "sportin' " lady before, being a married man, and I'll confess to being fascinated by the things she said. I should have been bone-tired from two months on the trail, but after my nap, the meal, and now the bourbon, I felt relaxed and uncommonly comfortable. There is something soft and nice about female company, and this pretty woman seemed to enjoy flirting with me. I wouldn't be honest if I said I wasn't flattered.

"You don't look like a cowpuncher," she observed.

I didn't know how to answer that, so I didn't say a thing.

She tossed her head a little, and ran her hand through a mass of dark, curly hair. She said, "You have a hard look about you. I don't know why—maybe it's your eyes. Anyone ever tell you how scary your eyes are?"

I frowned a little, offended.

"They're so pale, a very pale blue, and they look so cold." She laughed and put her hand on my arm. "Don't act so touchy. You know how attractive you are. Women must tell you that all the time."

I felt the blood rise to my face as I listened to the bell sounds of her laughter.

"What happened to the man who killed your husband?" I asked, trying to change the subject.

"Nothing. Nobody's fool enough to mess with J. K. Cade," she replied. When she saw my lack of understanding, she said, "You mean you haven't heard of him? Judas Priest! J.K. is bad news in anybody's book. God knows how many men he's killed. He carries a ten-gauge shotgun and a pistol half as long as your arm, and in the four years I've been here he's killed five men." She shook her head. "I'm scared silly of him, and so is everyone else."

He sounded like the type I'd like to give plenty of room. "He live in town?" I asked.

"No. He runs cattle southwest of here—has a place in a valley —but he comes to Black Horse every few weeks." Her eyes flashed with anger. "He comes mostly to see me—he thinks just because he pulled Jim Wichita off me that I'm his property, and I'm damn sick and tired of it."

The piano player came back to work, and began to pound away. I looked for the Texas boy I'd met earlier, but he and the little blond girl were nowhere in sight.

I put a silver dollar on the table to pay for our drinks, and stood up.

"You're not leaving, are you?" She sounded genuinely disappointed. "I don't often have the chance to sit with someone like you."

"I've been traveling a mighty long time," I said, returning her friendly smile.

As I walked toward the door, three cowboys got up from a table near it. One of them was about the size of an ox. His completely bald head looked shiny, and his forehead bulged out over his eyes. I don't believe I ever saw a bigger man—or an uglier one. He began to smack a huge bony fist into his ham hand. A cowboy with a greasy-looking brown hat stood beside him, hand on his six-gun, and a youngster moved right in front of me. It was the youngster who spoke.

"You're in trouble, mister. We seen you over yonder with Georgia Wichita."

The man with the greasy brown hat said in a flat voice, "We work for J. K. Cade, and that's his woman."

Rage jolted through me. It's something I'm not able to control, and I never know when it will strike. It's like something snaps inside my mind.

I whirled away from the two men on my right toward the kid who blocked my way. I only said one thing: "Stand aside."

The kid jerked a little and moved over toward the other two. I walked by them, trying to control the senseless fury. I told myself I wasn't armed. I told myself I'd come out this long way to start a new life, and I knew I'd have to fight my instincts as I'd never done before.

Walking down the dirt road beyond the board sidewalks I tried a few deep breaths, and that helped. None of this had a thing to do with Georgia Wichita. But it had plenty to do with a strong feeling I've had all my life. I won't be shoved.

CHAPTER FOUR

"This is a considerable sum, Mr. Germany," the banker said. He had introduced himself as Clyde Phillips, and he looked at me over his gold-rimmed spectacles with bright-eyed inquisitiveness. There is nothing like money to get a banker's attention. We sat in his small rectangular office which a wooden railing separated from the plank-floored bank lobby.

Backs of chairs, it occurred to me, were a waste for people like Clyde Phillips. He perched on the edge of his seat, and his pudgy hands fluttered nervously over a stack of papers like white butterflies unable to decide on which flower to light. I asked him not to mention the deposit or the fact that the cashier's check came from a bank in Santa Rita, Texas. He said, "It is a point of pride with me to be closemouthed," and then discussed this virtue of his for a full ten minutes.

Clyde Phillips assured me, his jowls quivering a little, "It takes a special breed of man to survive in Montana." He said with a touch of emotion, "Those of us who have made it here are hard men." He flushed with some pleasure, nodded his head, said again, "hard men," and set his weak jaw in a particularly grim way.

He polished his glasses and put them back on his nose. "It has only been eight years since the last great Indian battle took place in Montana. Chief Joseph of the Nez Percé surrendered to General Miles near Bear's Paw Mountain. I'm told Chief Joseph won all his battles but his last." He paused, relishing his words, enjoying the safe association of himself with a danger that lay in the past. "The Indians have been put on reservations north of the Missouri River, and since we've been free of them, my

word, how things have changed. The Northern Pacific Railroad
came through Montana in eighty-three, two years ago. The gold
miners were already here, but now we have copper miners too,
we have you cowmen—even some sheep raisers."

Wherever I have ridden in the West, I meet people trying to
be part of something they see slipping away. Strong men as well
as frail ones seem to see themselves in a peculiarly romantic
light, as though they're playing a role in a play or a long drama
about a time in history that somehow stands apart from other
times. I've watched men in filth and dirt and boredom who held
firmly to their pride in being a piece of something bigger than
themselves. They think they are having a hand in changing the
West, and I reckon they're right. Just to look at these dusty-
bearded men, hats squared over sunken eyes, sweaty shirts
usually buttoned to the neck to keep out the dirt and the wind,
you wouldn't consider them romantic. That morning I'd ridden
Ross around the town, wandered out to a ridge, and then returned. A man sat hunkered down beside the raw, new boards
of a shack that had a canvas top on it. No canvas sheltered the
crude privy behind it, though some boards and an old sign
formed walls that gave privacy, except maybe for a buzzard
gliding overhead. For no good reason I stopped my horse and
asked the man what he was doing. He didn't raise his eyes, but
he answered me. He said, "I'm watching the windmill turn and
the tank leak." It strikes me that for every liquid ounce of
romance in the West there is a good five gallons of hard work on
the one hand, and ten gallons of pure-dee boredom on the
other.

The banker's voice interrupted my thoughts. "I suppose you
know that you can't buy title to land here." He went into a
tirade, talking of the Montana Territory's government, using
words like "inept" and "corrupt" and worse. "Makes it hard to
plan for the future when some politician might sell your land
out from under you someday. On the other hand, while it lasts,
you have the best of all worlds, for the grass is *free.* It belongs to
the people of the United States, and to carve out a piece of it for

your own use, all you've got to do is put a notice in the nearest weekly newspaper; Butte has one and so does Helena. You list your brand, and describe the extent of your range." He spoke with careful emphasis: "But then you've got to hold it."

His bird eyes fixed on me. "I see you don't wear a gun. This territory has very little law except for vigilantes, and they can be worse than the bandits. You'll need guns, and you'll need men who carry them and can use them, I'm sorry to say."

I sensed a certain strength inside the fat little banker. There was more to him in all likelihood than I'd first assumed. Long ago I decided to reserve judgment on people, for I've often been wrong about my first impressions.

Clyde Phillips said, "The worst of the outlaws in my opinion is Bull Doggett. He and his gang have a hideout somewhere in the mountains west of here, and for several years they've been rustling cattle, holding up stagecoaches, and the like. His outfit is not the only one, of course. There is such lawlessness in the territory that I've gone to the expense of keeping an armed guard here at all times, day and night." He raised a hand and pointed toward a man sitting in a straight-backed chair tilted against a wall across the lobby. He held a rifle across his knees and wore a six-gun, and when anyone walked into the bank, he saw the man's eyes on him. I'll admit that he had given me a start when I'd entered the building.

The banker told me that only the week before a man who lived alone in a gulch not far away had been found murdered. He had been industrious; built a wooden flume to carry water to the spot where he had a placer mine. What little gold he may have found was gone, and he had been shot four times. Not only that, but he had been slashed badly—apparently by some kind of whip. "The savagery of it," Clyde Phillips said, shuddering, "is what makes this so horrible. We have no proof, but brutality is the trademark that Bull Doggett leaves behind. He must be crazy."

I had no answer to that, but I felt damned uneasy about walking around without my guns. In fact it made my skin crawl.

* * *

The people who ran the hotel had their own kitchen, and for a reasonable price prepared meals for guests staying there. Over a period of time their trade had grown, the owner told me, so now the small dining room had three tables in it, and during the short time of summer some folks carried their plates outside and ate on the porch.

I sat alone at my table inside, out of the cool wind, and listened while two women, apparently the wives of travelers, talked with considerable enthusiasm as they enjoyed their noonday meal. I've noticed that men who eat together rarely have much to say, but women find a meal someone else has cooked to be a celebration. Each one would wait with admirable restraint for the other to finish what she was saying, and then when her turn came, she spoke with renewed energy, giving great emphasis to the word "I."

The owner of the hotel, a man who had introduced himself to me the night before, came out, sweat showing through his shirt from being in the kitchen where they have a big black wood-burning stove. He sat down beside me with a glass of water, and he drank it slowly, eyes closed, savoring it. When he put it down, he sighed loudly.

"I seen you walking over here from the bank," he said.

I nodded.

He couldn't conceal his curiosity. "Planning to settle down here?"

"I'm not sure."

"Well, it's a fine place. Growing to beat the band."

He asked me what I thought of the banker, Clyde Phillips, and I didn't reply. So he informed me that Phillips was getting rich, what with his owning the only bank for many a mile, and loaning money to cowmen who wanted to buy stock at the ungodly interest rate of two percent a month.

That surprised me, and I guess it showed. The owner of the hotel said, "Yes sir, old Clyde has got the money," and then he added for no good reason, "and as everyone knows, money talks."

"Maybe it does," I replied, getting up to find a quieter spot to rest, "but it often doesn't have much to say."

He beamed at that, assuming that I joined him in the great brotherhood of men who despise the rich. As a matter of fact, many a person back home in Texas probably considers that I have more land, livestock, and money than any law ought to allow, and I've heard of people who hate me for that reason—even though they might never have met me. The long and short of it is simply this, a rich man can be as much a fool as a poor man, and that is all I really intended to say, but the hotel owner must have figured I had allied myself with him in his stand against the grasping bankers of the world.

A little later I walked down the street toward the town, thinking I'd look in on my horses. I'd given myself and them an extra day of rest before starting out to see Hap Cunningham. The banker, Clyde Phillips, knew Hap, and had told me where to find his ranch. He described it as lying in a wide valley north of here that formed a basin in the mountains. Hap had staked his claim under what Clyde Phillips described to me as "Montana's Law of Customary Range," which he said had been given informal recognition by the authorities of the territory since 1877.

I'd known the range was still free, but I hadn't counted on having to defend it against outlaws, or from new arrivals who might want to take the land I used away from me. I was thinking these thoughts while I walked toward the main part of the town. You'll never meet a cowboy who likes to walk, even for a short distance, and I was fuming about what a fool I'd been not to keep my horse at the hotel that afternoon. My boots scuffed through the ruts in the rough road that made up Black Horse's main street. In front of me I saw wagons with patient teams in front of stores while customers ambled here and there. Dogs darted underfoot, enjoying the confusion.

As I neared the buildings of the town, the three men who worked for J. K. Cade—the ones who had tried to threaten me the night before—came outside and began staring in my direction. The short man wearing a greasy brown hat walked over to where his horse stood hitched to the rail of the saloon. He pulled a rifle from its scabbard, and stepped back up on the sidewalk. He raised the rifle until he had me in his sights, but I kept walking toward him. A feeling of weakness hit my knees and worked its way up.

The rifle muzzle whipped down toward my feet and exploded. Dry, crusted mud flew up on my boots and pant legs. Needless to say, I stopped. Out of the corner of my eye I saw that all the people on the sidewalks did too. They stared curiously, wondering as I did what the hell was going on.

The big ox of a man, the one with a craggy, bald head, sidled off to my right, flexing his huge hands. He had a lopsided grin on his face as he stepped down off the sidewalk. Out of the corner of my eye I saw the youngster on my left, walking up the street toward me, his hand dangling by the butt of his six-shooter.

About that time the kid from Texas, Thatcher Stone, appeared and sauntered out of the saloon. He said, "Now, boys, three against one ain't fair."

The young cowboy before me jerked his hand to his gun, but Thatcher pulled his Colt .44 and leveled down on him. "Don't try anything like that, old son," he said with a stage voice that didn't sound like his. Maybe he had practiced it.

Thatcher had his pistol held high, and he stood right behind the man with the brown hat who'd been shooting close to my feet. This man started to turn around, but Thatcher caught him hard on the side of the head with his gun barrel, and the man flipped down and over the hitching rail. The three horses tied there reared, bucked, squealed more than whinnied, and then their reins broke and they clattered wildly down the street, running hell-bent for election.

Thatcher said in his quiet way, as if he were trying to reason with them, "Can't you boys see that my friend Mr. Germany don't have a gun on him?"

The ox had hunched over, great veins stood out on his bulging forehead, and a low rumble began in his throat. Thatcher said to him in what seemed to me to be a casual way, "Of course, you're not carrying a gun so I can't shoot you."

The ox began growling in a deep, murderous way. I complained to Thatcher, "I sure wish you hadn't said you wouldn't shoot him."

About then the growl turned into snarling noises, the ox lowered his head, and charged head down like a herd bull at the start of a fight. I stood for a second, glued to the spot. The big man moved quickly, head low, straight at me. At the moment of his dive, my knee came up and caught him square in the face.

In a contest between one man's nose and another man's knee, the knee is going to come out on top every damned time.

I felt the bone-jarring blow my knee gave, something crunched, and the ox-like man rolled on the mud beside the wooden water trough, hands to a face that spurted blood.

A sharp pain traveled up from my knee, but I forgot that, looking quickly to my left at the skinny young cowboy. He went for his gun, but Thatcher had moved down behind him, and he banged him over the head with his pistol barrel, just as he had with the one I identified as "Brown Hat." The cowboy's knees buckled, and he fell in a slump.

An old man with a white beard streaked brown and yellow with tobacco juice walked up, and he looked at the two still bodies of the men Thatcher had knocked out. Then he directed his attention to the giant bleeding all over the town's main street. The old man spat a long brown arc of tobacco juice, dribbled a fair amount of it down into his filthy beard, and said, "That's the most disgusting sight I ever seen."

He wiped his mouth on a caked shirt sleeve, and said wetly, "You boys are in for it now. All three of those men work for J. K. Cade, and that there," he pointed at the skinny cowboy who'd reached for his pistol before Thatcher had bashed him on the head, "is Jodie Cade, J.K.'s favorite nephew."

We looked at Jodie Cade, who rolled to his face, braced himself with his arms, then pulled himself up to his knees. He put his hand to the back of his head where he'd been hit, then brought it before his eyes. He looked up from his bloody fingers and the fury showed in his face.

Jodie Cade rose to his feet and fumbled for his pistol. I saw Thatcher Stone's face go deathly pale. He almost screamed when he cried out, "Don't try for it—don't do it."

Young Cade's gun came up, and Thatcher, holding his pistol in both hands, hollered, "No!"

Jodie's bullet bit a chunk of wood out of the wall beside Thatcher's head, and Thatcher's .44 roared. The slug hit the skinny young cowboy in the center of his chest, and he sat down hard. He looked at his chest, dumbfounded, and his mouth opened to form a question. Before he could ask it he fell backward, dead as a doornail.

"Jesus Christ!" the old man with the streaked beard yelled at Thatcher. This time I heard the terror in his voice. "Get out of town, boy, and do it quick. *Ride* before J. K. Cade finds you."

CHAPTER FIVE

We stood, frozen to the spot, and so did the wall of people that had formed around us by now.

Georgia Wichita threaded her way through the onlookers and touched my arm. "Get him out of town," she said. "Someone is on his way to J. K. Cade with the news."

Fine drops of sweat completely covered Thatcher's face in spite of the cool wind that swept over us. I've never seen a man look sicker. When I reached his side, I could see him shaking, and I said, "It's going to be all right. Let's go." Without saying another word I took hold of his elbow and pulled him along. He came without protest.

We went to the hotel where I packed my things, paid my account, and left hurriedly for the livery stable. Thatcher stayed close beside me throughout all of this. By the time I'd saddled Joe, I could see that Thatcher had regained his composure. He told me he had spent the night with the blond girl, a touch of pride in his voice, and he said he had his belongings already tied in his bedroll. We led our horses out of the stables and began to mount. As Thatcher put his weight on the stirrup, his roman-nosed horse snaked his head back to bite him. He slapped at the horse and stepped into the stirrup again, but the next thing he knew his rump hit the dust, for the saddle slipped clear around on his horse's side. The cantankerous animal had swelled up out of a sense of inborn peevishness when the cinch was fastened.

Furious, Thatcher jumped up, slammed his knee into his horse's side, which made the irritable creature grunt and breathe out, which allowed the girth to be cinched up tight.

He remounted, holding long reins down loose in his left hand, trying to look nonchalant as though nothing had happened. It struck me that this cowboy seemed to pose a lot. He pushed his hat up and leaned back lazily. About that time the roman-nosed horse decided to get even. His back bowed up, his head went down between his feet, and it was Katie-bar-the-door from then on. He bounded high and came down on stiff legs which jolted him back up as if he had a belly full of bedsprings. He bucked down the road beside the livery stable, behind a house next door, and then through a clothesline. Dripping, long-handled underwear and women's wet, flapping garments draped around Thatcher's face caused him to lose his balance, not to mention his concentration, and the first thing you knew he'd been thrown. Somehow he held on to the reins, and in a rage got back into the saddle as his crazy horse whipped in circles trying to keep him off. With the clothesline and the washing out of the way he stayed on until his horse got tired of pitching. Then, red-faced and embarrassed, Thatcher joined me where I sat on Joe with Ross behind on the lead rope.

We rode in silence until I said, "That's a very valuable horse you've got there. Many a man with troubles has to sit and worry about them, but with a mount like yours there's no time for that."

The next morning we left camp at first light. We'd been forced to stop when it got dark the night before. For a time we'd tried to find our way through the strange mountains, but it soon became evident that we'd better pull up. Thatcher had called it to my attention by saying, "Tom, I do believe we're getting loster and loster."

By the first rays of the dawn we backtracked, clattering over rocks and a few fallen trees until we found the trail again that led north through the mountain passes. There was no sign of pursuit.

At midday we watered the horses at a clear, cold river. The shallow water rushed over smooth stones making splashing noises. As we stood there a most remarkable thing happened.

Upstream an elk approached the river with elegant grace, his immense antlered head raised high. The sight captivated me. I've hunted whitetail and blacktail deer all my life, but I'd never seen anything like this. A fully grown bull elk is taller than a horse, and this one had a widespread set of antlers. The animal saw us and stopped an instant, head up—alert. Then, carefully —almost daintily—he stepped forward as though curious. At that moment Thatcher's rifle rang out, and the elk dropped to his knees. The sound of the rifle reverberated again through the rocks and trees of the narrow valley, and the elk slid down to his side—dead, but with his large brown eyes still open.

Dismayed, I turned to see Thatcher, his face hot, full of the blood lust of the hunt.

"Why in hell would you do a thing like that? We can't stop to skin him. There's no time for it," I stormed at the young man, aghast at what he had done. Men have hunted through the centuries, it's born in us, but *we kill to live.* We shouldn't kill anything, man or beast, for any other reason. I said in a cold way, "If there are men behind us, the sound of your shots has given us away."

"I'm sorry, Tom," Thatcher said, as flustered as a kid. "It all happened so fast. . . ."

We mounted, and as soon as we reached level ground, I put my horse into a high lope, and fought against my feelings of anger at the waste of the elk's life. After a while we fell back to a regular trot.

"You still mad?" Thatcher asked, his tone hesitant, as though he were a ten-year-old.

I had to smile. "No, I'm not," I replied, and as a matter of fact it was true. I have a tendency to flare up, but then I'm usually able to forget it.

"I just didn't think," Thatcher said, and I told him that was the damn truth. Then I proceeded to give him holy hell for a few minutes. That led me to telling him some of the fool things I'd done at his age. I'm not that much older than he is, but I sure feel as though I am. Part of it is being married and having a child, I suppose. He laughed at a crazy tale I told, and I started laughing too. The explosion of a rifle firing put an end to that in a hurry. It made that awful, flat "whap" sound, the way it does when a bullet goes immediately over your head. Without a word being necessary between us, we slammed our spurs into our horses' sides and they leaped forward into a dead run. Another shot hit a boulder to my right and ricocheted in a wild, screaming whine. More shots buzzed past us as we leaned forward over our horses' necks.

I rode Ross, and when he opened up, it felt as if I was on a locomotive with a full head of steam on a downhill grade. I had dropped the lead rope, but Joe ran beside us with long, bounding muscular strides. I looked over my shoulder and it seemed Thatcher was standing still, although of course he was doing his dead-level best to keep up. Behind him, bursting into the clearing beside the river, I saw five mounted men racing in pursuit.

The trail at the end of the narrow valley led to an open basin on the left. I slowed up, waiting for Thatcher. Thousands of lush green acres swelled out before me, protected on three sides by soaring mountains. It fit the description of Hap Cunningham's ranch I'd been given by the banker. To the right I could see a pass between the mountains, and I figured that the trees there would give us good protection.

I pulled up sharply and stepped down, dropping the reins. In West Texas we train our horses to stand, and a good one always will. Joe came to me when I held out my hand, and then Thatcher pounded up. I had no time to explain, much less to argue. When he questioned me, I pulled him off his horse, and without a word unsaddled and unbridled the roman-nosed brute, which stood there—heaving away, legs spraddled out— during the process.

In no more than about a minute I'd saddled Joe for Thatcher Stone, and his former mount galloped off, no doubt delighted to be free.

Thatcher beamed with pleasure as he stepped into the saddle. With both of us on good horses we set off into a run again, and when our pursuers came in sight, it was clear that they were falling behind rapidly. Moments later we entered the trees and headed east, settling into a gallop with some difficulty by hauling back on the reins, for Joe and Ross still had it in their heads to run. After a spell I chose a long, traveling trot that eats up the ground. Both of our horses could keep this going all day long, and I expected that the cow ponies behind us would have to be in a slow lope to keep up. And they couldn't do that for very long without wearing clear out.

"There's no sign of them," I said. We had left the trail hours before, and now the night spread out around us black as pitch. We dismounted and made camp.

"Damnedest two horses I ever seen in all my born days," Thatcher Stone declared for at least the tenth time. "What I don't understand is how you can travel with two studs. Don't they ever fight?"

"Joe has a good disposition, but it took a while for Ross to get used to the idea of traveling at the end of a rope, regardless of whether he was the lead or the trail horse. But I figured on that and have a quirt at all times on my saddle horn, as you probably noticed. Whenever Ross gets out of hand I have to quirt him a time or two, and he quietens down. He's a smart animal, and it doesn't take us long to get our differences straightened out."

Then I told him why I had traveled from Texas with two stallions, explaining my dream of starting a small ranch. I talked a little concerning my plan to catch some of the best mares in the big herds of wild horses that roam these parts, an idea that seemed to captivate Thatcher. Afterward I told him about Santiago coming with four cowboys, the chuck wagon driver, extra mounts for the men and teams for the wagon, and—most important of all—the fifteen mares that we had carefully chosen. In time, I said, we hoped with careful crossbreeding to establish a fine herd.

"Man alive," Thatcher said, looking excited, "that sure sounds like a lot of fun. I sure would enjoy seeing the rodeo when you begin trying to break those wild mustangs."

I told him that it might be best for him to head back to Texas, since he had gotten off on the wrong foot in Montana. But Thatcher said he'd be damned if he'd leave. I told him he might be damned if he stayed.

"It's just one man," he said, although his voice didn't sound near as confident as his words.

"Looked to me like there were five shooting at us," I replied.

"But if I get J. K. Cade, the others will back off."

"You never know," I responded. Then I said, "Thatcher, I don't know whether this man Cade is a real gunfighter or not. There are those who get the name through being meaner than other folks. Some of them aren't all that good with their guns—but they don't hesitate when it comes to killing a man. Most decent people are going to hesitate." I didn't say much more, but he knew I was talking about his actions in the fight in Black Horse.

He colored and said, "I've faced a gunslinger before and walked away from it. In fact, that's how come I've got these gold coins in the chain around the crown of my hat. Had to shoot a Meskin name of the Juarez Kid."

I sat there a little and didn't say a word. There are a good many Mexicans in Texas, and some of them are very close friends of mine. I know a little about how they think, and not any self-respecting Mexican would call himself by a gringo name like that. After a little the silence got to be more than Thatcher could bear. He coughed, and with a second effort said, "Well, at least that's what some fellows I know used to call him."

I still didn't say anything. Finally Thatcher's third version developed. He said, "What really happened is that I was in the pasture one day, cowboyin' near Valentine. This barefooted Mexican came by and told me he was speeding to the bedside of his ailing mother in Chihuahua." Thatcher began to chuckle at the idea of a man on foot speeding anywhere. "The long and short of it is that I ended up trading him a wind-broke horse for his hat chain." He apologized for wandering from the truth. I told him I didn't know if he'd recognize the truth if it was staring him straight in the face. Thatcher grinned and said, "You'll have to admit it made a better story the way I told it first."

I've known people before who would rather lie than tell the truth, even when there's no reason for it. Others try hard to get people to believe they are what they'd *like* to be. I hadn't known Thatcher long enough to decide if he belonged in one or both of these categories. Maybe he was just trying to impress me, which is not an uncommon thing for a young fellow to do. I don't suppose many men can say that they didn't do their share of showing off when they were coming of age.

My companion broke in on my thoughts. He spoke shyly. "Tom, back home my family and my good friends call me Buddy. I'd be obliged if you'd call me that."

"I'll be happy to, although I've only known you a few days, and am just getting used to connecting the name 'Thatcher' with you."

He looked embarrassed for some reason, so I assured him I'd do my dead-level best to remember to call him Buddy, but not to be upset if I forgot. As a matter of fact I never could bring myself to call him that, for I'd already got the name "Thatcher" fixed in my mind.

It was cold as all get-out, but we didn't dare light a fire. Whenever we heard the wind make tree branches crack against each other, both of us would jump up, rifle in hand. It's hard to sleep when you know five armed men are on the hunt for you.

CHAPTER SIX

We hid for three days, living on beef jerky at first. Then Thatcher Stone pulled some fishing line and hooks from his saddlebags, put grasshoppers on the hooks, and broke off a slender tree branch which he smoothed with his knife. He peeled the bark off and soon fashioned a six-foot-long, whippy fishing pole. After half a day of tromping up and down beside a creek which ran directly by our camp, he caught three big trout—one right after another. Thatcher hollered with pleasure each time his limber pole doubled under the weight of the arching, silvery fish. They leaped from the water into the air through rainbowed spray, tails twisting, and he had to fight to land them. If the gunmen after us had been nearby, we'd have been discovered without any question. I told Thatcher that when you hide from people intent on killing you, it would be best not to howl like a red Indian, since that might possibly give you away.

We took a chance and built a small cooking fire, and I must say that I've never tasted anything better than those trout.

"I guess things look bad," Thatcher said after discussing the number of men after us.

"Try to remember that the sky is always darkest just before fire, flood, pestilence, and earthquakes," I replied.

"It ain't funny to me," he protested. "You can joke all you want to, it's *my* hide that J. K. Cade's really after. And all because of you."

I apologized and told him that I did appreciate his helping me out when the three men jumped me in Black Horse. I said, "I still haven't figured why they would do such a thing."

Thatcher reminded me, "They warned you that woman belonged to J. K. Cade."

"The lady sure didn't see herself as his property. But be that as it may, it would be ridiculous for us to get shot over a woman," I fumed. "I'm married and settled down, and I certainly didn't make a play for Georgia Wichita the other night."

Thatcher Stone said, "I was in the saloon the day after I met you, and those three men came in. The young one, Jodie Cade, acted riled because the others teased him about jumping to one side when you ordered him out of your way the night before. As a matter of fact, they all seemed embarrassed that you flared up at them and made them back down. I reckon that's why they decided to teach you a lesson. But one thing led to another and . . ." His voice trailed off.

I had been watching him carefully as he spoke. I saw him wince when he mentioned the name of Jodie Cade, for he had carefully avoided that matter ever since we'd been in hiding. I sighed. One thing certainly did lead to another, as Thatcher had observed. A stiff-backed order from me, hurt pride on the part of those cowboys, and then a ruckus that ended with Thatcher's bullet dropping Jodie Cade. What a hell of a way to start my new life in Montana!

The next morning we rode back down the trail to the west, and before noon reached the basin we'd glimpsed when we had been in a dead run. We saw no sign of our pursuers. Both of us felt a little edgy, and we kept looking around.

"Look, Tom, over yonder," Thatcher cried out, pointing to a fold in the skirts of a mountainside.

I had my Winchester out after his first cry, but then I saw the object of his attention. About a hundred horses trailed over the long ridge leading up toward the big mountain on our right. The horses filed out of sight, and a fine-looking black stallion stood at a high point off to one side, waiting until they were safe. Then, tail and mane flared out, he jumped through rocks with the agility of a mountain goat and disappeared after them.

"My God," Thatcher said. "What a sight."

I agreed heartily.

An hour later we came across wagon tracks, and followed them until late afternoon. They led into a long valley with a swift mountain river swirling through it. We crossed this at a shallow place where the wagon had forded. A little later we crested a rise, and down below us we spied a large two-story house built of logs with mortar plastered between them. It had stone chimneys at each end, and porches with railings in front of them across the entire front of the house on the ground floor and also upstairs. Thick wooden shingles covered the roof. We drew closer and I made out chairs on the porches, and on the walls behind them I saw deer and elk horns hanging here and there.

Hap Cunningham walked from a big barn which lay off to one side and behind the house, shading his eyes as he examined us. He wore galluses to hold his britches up over his big stomach, and as usual had his pants legs tucked in his boots.

A big grin slowly creased his face. "Well, I'll be a sonuvabitch if it ain't Tom Eng . . ."

"Howdy, Hap," I broke in to keep him from saying my name. I jumped off my horse and rushed to him, and as he gave me a bear hug, I told him, "Remember that out here I'm called Tom Germany."

Hap remedied his blunder when I introduced him to Thatcher Stone, saying that any friend of Tom Germany's was a friend of his.

Polly Cunningham, Hap's wife, roared out her howdies to Thatcher and me. She hadn't changed much, except her hair might have gone a little grayer. It used to be red. Polly possessed a voice that carried. She could in all likelihood outholler a steam engine's whistle if she was a mind to. And you never had to wonder what was on her mind, for she would tell you. Her son Jeff, a gawky good-natured seventeen-year-old, smiled in a shy way as he joined us. The boy must have stood about six feet three, and was as awkward as a newborn colt, all legs and elbows.

I had written to Hap and Polly that I was coming, and about my reasons for it. In the letter I asked them to help me begin a new life out in Montana under the name of Tom Germany, and I was relieved when neither Polly nor their son gave me away.

Polly served us a supper of beef together with frijoles from a large black iron pot which Polly kept, Texas style, at the back of her stove at all times. Then we sat in the living room while Jeff built up a fire for us. I told Hap what had happened in Black Horse, and he liked to have died laughing until I came to the part about Thatcher having to shoot Jodie Cade. He listened to the rest of the story with growing restlessness.

"Trouble has followed you, Tom, since you were a little kid," he said grimly. He got up with some effort and went to the kitchen. He returned with his whiskey bottle and two glasses. Polly left us for her kitchen, saying she wanted to clean things up, and Jeff took Thatcher out to the bunkhouse to meet the cowboys who worked on the place.

Hap and I sat in his plank-floored living room in two ladder-back rocking chairs. A colorful rag rug brightened the room, and the yellow flickering of flames in the stone fireplace warmed it. An old Henry rifle with a scarred stock hung on a rack over the mantel, and a worn, flat-horned Mexican saddle with heavy tapaderos over the stirrups for protection from thorny trees and bushes lay stiffly on its side in a corner. Hap and I cradled glasses of bourbon as we rocked from time to time, creaking comfortably. After bringing each other up to date, Hap stood up and went to the desk behind us. He pawed through a drawer, talking to himself, then found what he sought. He returned and held something out to me.

Hap said, "I ran across this the last time I was in Black Horse. Found it in the hotel lobby—guess a traveler left it behind. Anyway, I figured you ought to see it." Then he added, "This magazine has circulated pretty widely out here since the Northern Pacific Railway came through." He handed me a magazine entitled *Chicago Weekly*, with a subtitle in a drawing of the sun's rays which said, "A Journal of America's Westward Expansion."

I looked up, wondering, and Hap said, "You'll see what caught my attention on the third page."

On turning to it I saw my image staring me in the face. I've seen crude drawings of me in the papers before, but this likeness was uncanny. Small type above the picture stated: "Wood engraving from gelatin-silver print of photograph." Then I remembered the man with the cumbersome wooden camera box who took my picture at our Fourth of July party at the ranch almost a year before. I had stood in dark pants and a white shirt against a tree. The photographer had crouched down to get the angle he wanted, and he kept cautioning me to be still—not to move a muscle. It all came back.

In the illustration my arms were folded across my chest as I stared grimly into the lens. The figure in the picture looked forbidding, menacing—a six-gun hanging low on each leg. Under the engraving, a painstaking copy of the photograph which was a marvel of accuracy to my eye, ran the caption, "Tom English, the Most Dangerous Man Alive."

I stared at this, dumbfounded. Hap said he had to check on his wife, that he'd be back in a few minutes, and walked out of the room, leaving me alone to read the magazine.

I shifted my chair closer to the lamp, and turned its wick up to get more light. Then I addressed myself to the article, noting every word in it with care.

THE MASTER GUNFIGHTER
by George Lindstrom

On April 6, 1885, in Santa Rita, Texas, Joe Logan sought to become known in history as the man who finally shot down the notorious Tom English, but instead ended as his 21st victim.

Dozens of news articles and two books have been written about English, but the questions remain: Who is this man?

What motivates him? I have come to the conclusion that he is a natural warrior who has perfected his deadly skills until he is the most dangerous man alive.

This reporter over the past six years has made numerous trips throughout the American West researching a strange and terrible reality: the craft and art of gunfighting as practiced in our frontier states during the last fifteen years. I have interviewed witnesses of dozens of gun battles and duels. I have read a great many newspaper accounts and probably all of the books written about this phenomenon, and I submit that a dangerous subculture has appeared in our nation that is a throwback to the ancient days of jousting in England, and of duels there and in France in bygone centuries.

A curious hierarchy develops in dueling cults. After many bloody contests a champion emerges, and then those who seek recognition must overthrow him. We could liken it to a child's game of "king of the mountain" were it not so tragic, for the loser in dueling ordinarily is not simply pushed aside. He is killed.

Gunfights are usually random, crude affairs where luck and brutality play a very large part. We might compare them with ancient battles between combatants armed with broadswords or maces. As in the past certain skilled men rose above this and became fencing masters, so now we see the rise of a special breed of man for whom armed conflict with revolvers has been transformed into a "discipline."

In France one hundred years ago there lived a few master swordsmen, skilled at thrust and parry, who were deadly when they entered on the dueling fields. Only men of like skills could hope to survive against them. The manual and physical dexterity and the required viciousness to kill an opponent without mercy were important. But in those days one other element was always present: the honing of natural skills to the highest possible degree by constant, dedicated practice. In our century the only classical duelist who has emulated the masters of the past, although probably unconsciously, is Tom English. He has taken this extra step so as to raise his inherent, native abilities to almost superhuman levels.

By devoting hours every day to the practice of drawing his twin six-guns with either left or right hand, he has reached a point where each "hand is quicker than the eye." At least ten men who have personally seen this genius of death in action have given me their testimony on this score. In addition to his breathtaking quickness, his shooting accuracy is astonishing. Many witnesses over the years have attested to that. A small cemetery could be filled with the victims who give their own mute testimony from the grave. For them the twin Colts he wears were "terrible swift swords."

Joe Logan of Cuero, Texas, probably didn't think through the fact that he was part of a "dueling cult"; but he surely must have acted from reasons he would have had difficulty in explaining when he sought out Tom English in order to kill him. He had never once met the man. No reason could possibly justify his actions other than the one set forth above. Many people observed what happened, and I have spoken to them. English held a glass of whiskey in his right hand when Logan aimed at his back, fired, and missed. To a man, the people watching swear that at the explosion of Logan's gun Tom English drew and fired with his left hand before Joe Logan could squeeze his trigger a second time. I submit that no other man alive could have survived this attack.

The legendary duelist has disappeared from his sprawling ranches in West Texas. Efforts to find him for an interview have been fruitless. He is riding alone somewhere in the West, like a wolf circling frightened cattle. He is riding alone, heavily armed and very dangerous. The defenders of order have every right to be deeply concerned. He is not sought by the authorities, for he has broken no laws, but the fact remains that wherever this man has been—bloodshed and violence have followed. This is his lot. This is the life— while it lasts—of Tom English, Master Gunfighter.

Well, I thought, George Lindstrom got part of it right. He couldn't have known about Mary Dawson's hiring Logan to shoot me. However, there's no reason to complain about newspapers or magazines because their writers don't have all the facts. Few, if any, people do.

I saw nothing new in the article except for the writer's strange conclusions. He could never know how it all started— when Jack Malone pointed his shotgun at my belly when I was a kid of seventeen. Hell, *naturally* I practice. I'm too scared not to. And while it's true I've been riding alone, I certainly shouldn't be compared to some wolf prowling around a frightened herd. I'm too busy looking over my shoulder for other wolves who are after *me*.

Hap came back in the room. "I suspect you found that to be interesting, Tom."

"Yes, I did," I responded a little more tersely than I should.

"Don't get testy with me; I didn't write it."

"I know that, Hap. My question is this: how can I find any peace when those newspaper writers keep chivvying the youngsters with such stories. It's almost like they want to goad them into coming after me."

"They have to sell newspapers, don't they? If they build you into a 'legend,' they'll have thousands of people interested in what happens to you. Since the war ended, they haven't had many heroes or villains to write about. You may look like a hero to some, and a villain to others—and the stories will sell papers. Not much doubt about that."

"Seems like a strange way to make a living," I mused, and Hap agreed.

"Tomorrow," Hap said, "I'll take you and your young friend out to see some of those mustangs you were talking about. It would be a relief for me to get some of them off my range. As you know, I only aim to raise cattle, and as far as I'm concerned, the only thing those damned animals are good for is to eat my grass."

"They fascinate me, Hap, and I've read all I can find about them. From what I've been able to learn, the mustangs developed into a breed of their own from horses brought over from Spain hundreds of years ago by the conquistadors. They're all over the West now, of course, but those up here, I'm told, are different. An old-timer I met on the trail when I was traveling from Texas claimed that the Nez Percé Indians in the Northwest, in fact where Montana is now, developed a line of gray, spotted horses that are fine specimens."

"Sounds like what we call Appaloosas," Hap said, "but I don't know nothing about Indians working with their horses. On the other hand, that tribe you mentioned may have in the past. I'm sorely afraid that what you see will disappoint you. From what I hear, the Indians as a general rule took the best studs for their riding horses and left the runts uncut, so they were free to reproduce. That's one reason why most of those mustangs are so small. I would say they average just thirteen hands in height, and most of them are sorry-looking. As a rule you'll find they are hammer-headed and ewe-necked. I've seen them all too often, Tom, and you wouldn't have the average one as a gift. They're tied-in below the knee, mutton-withered, roach-backed, and cow-hocked. And this is what you find fascinating?"

"Hap, I'm sure that what you say is so, but Thatcher and I saw some beautiful mares being herded by a black stallion on our way to your place, so there must be some exceptions. I read that the mustangs came originally from Spanish horses with Arab and Barb blood; and even you will have to admit that they're tough and live well on their own. If we take the time to select the best mustang mares, and if we can catch a few good stallions, we can cross them with our horses, and in time build up

what is in a way our own strain." The more I talked about it the
more excited I got.

Hap looked at me with that skeptical way of his, as though I'd
lost my damn mind, and finally he said, "Well, I wish you luck. I
particularly hope you can catch that big black stud. That sonuvabitch has raided my remuda time and again, and has run off
with some of my best mares. My boys have tried to corral them,
but they can't get close. If you manage it, I want you to return
any horseflesh wearing the HC brand."

Hap told me to stay in Jeff's room that night, since his son
preferred the bunkhouse. He noted the pleasure Jeff had shown
when Thatcher showed up with me, for Hap's cowboys were all
grown men. "Young folks are like old folks," Hap remarked.
"We all like to be around people of our own age."

Then Hap said, "I'm worried about that magazine article,
Tom. The picture in it is an excellent likeness of you. You'd best
not go into town until you grow a beard. It wouldn't be safe. In
addition, you better let things cool down where J. K. Cade is
concerned."

CHAPTER SEVEN

"You planning to sleep your life away?" Hap bawled through the door at me.

I sat bolt upright in the bed, not knowing where I was—frightened and weak—the way you can be very early in the morning.

"What time is it?" I asked, uncertainly.

"Must be four o'clock. Come on down, the coffee's ready."

Hap didn't have to tell me that. His big black coffeepot never left the stove. I rolled out of the bed, and as I did, the fear faded. I almost forgot it. The chill morning air made me shiver, and I hurried into my clothes, then slid on my boots.

When I reached the kitchen, Hap said, "We'll have our first cup here before we go to the bunkhouse. Luther Hawkins, our cook, is fixing breakfast for the boys down there, and I generally eat with them." Then he said, "Today we're going to check on our stock, and it takes an early start to do it. This place isn't large by Texas standards, but some of it is rough country, so the cattle aren't easy to find."

I sat down at the heavy pine table, feeling the warmth of the stove at my back, and ducked my head toward the steaming mug of coffee. The darkness outside crowded up close to the windows, and the lamp in the kitchen cast an unnaturally bright circle of light.

Hap said, "My ranch has three natural divisions. We've got five or six thousand acres in what I call the Basin, maybe two thousand acres here in the Valley sector, and at least seven thousand in the Mountains. I've got my eye on a fourth area that isn't part of my claim yet. It lays to the east of my mountain pastures. A pass leads to it from there, and some of my strays wander into it once in a while." He said, "I've got a special reason for discussing all of this with you."

He opened a leather folder and pulled out a sheaf of papers. "I paid Ernest Claybrook a good price for his cattle and horses, as well as for this house when I came to Montana three years ago. Ernest had been here four years, and had done a good job. But he was getting along in years and his health was failing, so he sold out. He never quite recovered from the drive up here from Texas. What with one thing and another it took him nine months, although naturally that included some long stops. He had some good stories to tell about that trip. He started with over two thousand head of cattle and drove them all the way from Texas up the Chisholm Trail to Kansas, then to Ogallala, Nebraska, and finally to this range in Montana. He had some terrible luck crossing all the rivers that lay across his way, and lost some cattle as well as men to Indians." Hap mused, "We've come a long way since those days. A man would hardly recognize this country," he said with some pride. "At any rate Ernest Claybrook managed to get here with eight hundred and ninety head of cattle."

Hap drank some coffee, and then spread out a page filled with figures on the table. "Ernest kept good records, and I've stayed with the system he developed for the sake of consistency. As each year passes I'm able to appreciate his methods more, for by looking at what happened in the past I'm able to anticipate what the future holds. If you'll look at this, you'll see for yourself what has happened, and the surprising thing that I think is *going* to happen."

I examined the table of carefully penciled numbers which he laid before me with interest.

Years	Steers	Yearlings	Cows	Born	Total
1st	190	190	300	290	970
2nd	90	290	400	300	1,080

3rd	80	300	970	400	1,750
4th	100	400	720	600	1,820
5th	190	500	1,070	800	2,660
6th	200	800	1,470	1,000	3,470
7th	300	1,000	2,070	1,600	4,790

Projected Outlook for the Next Three Years Based on Above Experience:

8th	500	1,600	2,870	2,500	7,470
9th	790	2,500	4,100	4,000	11,390
10th	1,000	4,000	6,000	9,900	21,000

"If you'll study that," Hap said, "you'll see my best guess as to what ought to happen in the next three years. If I'm right, my herd will jump from forty-seven hundred to twenty-one thousand head. I'm not shy about telling you that such a thing as that scares the living hell out of me. I ran twelve to sixteen hundred cows on my little place near Sonora when I lived in Texas, and I'm comfortable with that size operation. But this thing is getting clear out of hand. I got a bear by the tail and I've got to hang on, though I feel that I should climb a tree and find safety. What I'm leading up to is this, I'm going to need some help."

I studied his calculations, fascinated. I asked, "About this figure on yearlings . . ."

He broke in, knowing my question before I asked it, "That includes both steer and cow calves under a year old."

"You're only selling your steers after they are old enough to carry some weight," I observed. He nodded. "What is involved in getting them to market?" I asked.

"There's always some awkwardness about that, no matter where you ranch. But this place, for all that it seems out on the edge of the earth, is one hell of a lot easier to ship from than any ranch you'll find in Texas, and that is one of its big advantages. Aside, of course, from having plenty of free range." A hint of a smile ghosted across his face.

Hap Cunningham said, "In Texas you're faced with driving

your herd for months to Kansas to the railroad. The buyers
there know they are going to have the expense of shipping the
cattle to market, so they make allowances for that when they set
the prices they are willing to pay. All we have to do is drive our
steers to either Bozeman or Billings right here in Montana.
They are both set up with pens and chutes for loading right onto
the railcars. It takes us from ten days to two weeks after our
roundup to get to the shipping point, but then the Northern
Pacific Railway carries our beef to Chicago in only six or seven
days. And I reckon that Chicago is the best market you can find.
Even though an average steer loses from a hundred and twenty
to a hundred and sixty pounds on the trip, he still will weigh an
average of nine hundred pounds on arrival. We've been selling
for five cents a pound lately, although occasionally we hit a bad
market and only sell at three and a half cents. But we average
just at thirty-five dollars a head. It is a very good, a very profit-
able business."

Outside a rooster began to crow, but as yet no hint of dawn
lightened the night sky. Hap spread his rough hands out on the
table and said, "You can see that this herd is growing faster than
I'm going to be able to handle. I'm faced with establishing a
much larger ranch than I've ever handled, or I've got to sell off
some of the herd to keep it about the size it is now. A third
approach would be to get some help. That's what I'm leading up
to with you."

Hap leaned back in his chair with a lazy half smile on his face.
Then he continued. "We've been friends for years, Tom, and
I've kept track of the things you've done. You have the capital
and the know-how when it comes to a big cattle operation. This
ranch has a good start, and the probability of large growth. If
you're interested, I'll sell you a half interest in everything I've
got here for one hundred and fifty thousand dollars. That
amount will mean security for my wife and Jeff if something
should happen to me. From your standpoint, it's less than market price for the cattle alone. The horses, this house and the
barns and corrals and improvements, together with the equip-

ment I bought from Ernest Claybrook or have added in the last three years—all that is thrown in. The reason I'm making this proposition to you, Tom, is that my half of the partnership down the road could be worth a sight more than if I start selling off my mother cows now. It gives me a way to have my cake and eat it too, for I'll get all my capital out, and will be riding free and clear as we build things up. I would have made that table run out another five years, but the figures got too wild." He concluded by saying that an abundance of free grass made one hell of a difference in the way people made their calculations when it came to the costs of ranching.

I said, "You sure know how to get a man's attention, Hap. I came up here to find a little horse ranch, and in five minutes you've come close to changing my direction."

"I don't want you to think I'm putting any pressure on you, Tom. In fact, I wouldn't have brought the matter up if I hadn't thought it was more than fair for both of us. But I would ask you not to give me any decision until you have ridden over the ranch for a few weeks—or for that matter, as long as you like. Naturally, you should look over the cattle too, and if you want to, we can gather them and get a good count."

I thanked him, and then he asked if I had any questions. I asked, "What do you figure your costs run per year for each head?"

"They'll be in the range of seventy-five cents, I'd say. We pay more for cowhands than you might in Texas, what with the Mexicans who hire on with you. Because of the mountains and the nature of the country here, we might have to use more men per thousand head than you would on the plains. But then one big cost you've got, which is the money you've got in your land, is zero in our case."

Hap said, "Let me go over what we pay our help. Cowboys start at thirty dollars a month with board. Experienced hands might earn more, and some of the top men, those who can handle responsibility, could earn as much as ninety dollars. Naturally they get food, lodging, horses to ride, and the like. All they need to do is bring their own saddle. I've no use for a man who would sell his saddle. None at all." Hap snorted at the very idea.

"My experience," Hap said, "shows me that it is false economy to have less than two cowboys for twelve hundred to fourteen hundred cattle. I've only got four men now plus my foreman. But in three years' time I'll be faced with the need to employ at least seventeen cowboys, which would include several head honchos to be in charge of the ranch's different divisions. It goes without saying that—to handle the stock—we'd have to add a good bit of land."

Hap rose and said, "I couldn't ask for a better man than you as a partner. As I said before, you need to take the time to think this over, for it has to be something that would be in your own best interests. It just looks to me like a situation where everybody is better off, where it's an advantage on your part and mine too. Regardless of what you choose to do, I want you to know that I won't think any the less of you if you decide against my offer."

I thanked him, feeling awkward as you do when someone pays you a compliment. Then we went to the bunkhouse where Hap presented me to his men. Thatcher sat off to one side, grousing about having to get up in the middle of the night, but he was in a good humor, and I could tell he was looking forward to seeing the ranch.

Hap said, "You know our foreman. You cowboyed with him at Jason Field's Lower Ranch about ten years ago."

A bowlegged man with a long, drooping mustache came up and held his hand out to me.

"Stafford Darnell! I wouldn't have thought of you for ten dollars."

He grinned at me with what teeth he had left. Except for his mustache having turned iron-gray, he looked much as he had when I'd last seen him. We sat together at the long trestle table after filling our plates, and I received a formal introduction to Luther Hawkins, the ranch cook. The old man had a cranky look about him, but I could tell that he was looking to see if we liked what he prepared. When I had first walked in, I had watched him mixing a fresh batch of biscuits in the top of his heavy flour sack which sat propped up against the wall next to the stove. These were baking now while we made inroads on the loaded platters which he had placed before us. In addition, we each had a slab of beef, and thin gravy to pour over our biscuits. The smell of the food and of coffee filled the room. The men gave voice to the kind of early morning complaints you expect from a bunch of cowboys; and several of them looked at me curiously. The bunkhouse where we sat was a log-walled building with the kitchen at one end and a line of wooden bunks with thin mattresses at the other. The stove sat in the middle of the floor toward the section with beds, and served to divide the two areas as well as to heat the place at night.

Stafford and I sat at one end of the table where we could talk privately. He said, "Hap told me you were headed this way, Tom. Hear you're using a new name, so I reckon they're after you." His long-handled mustache hung down below his jaw on both sides, and it gave him a mournful appearance. "I'm glad you came up here to bid us good-bye before the law hangs you."

I grinned at him. "Stafford, I swear I'm innocent."

He said, "Innocent, my foot. You got the look of a man fleeing justice." Then he changed the subject. "You remember Thelma, I expect," he said, referring to his wife.

I nodded. No one forgot Thelma. She was as ugly as home-made sin some men argued, while others claimed that was going too far, although they admitted she might be considered to be a little common, maybe as common as pig tracks. Regardless of the names folks called Thelma, she had a way of growing on you.

"Thelma," Stafford said, "like to of had a fit when I drug her out here. She hollered that it was the Lord's judgment on her for marrying a sinful cowboy instead of that God-fearing drummer from Fort Worth. But now, although she wouldn't admit it, she has fallen in love with Montana."

Hap pulled up a chair at the end of the table so he could join us. He had heard the end of the conversation and he said, "Thelma is good company for Polly."

"Thelma has grown a little hard of hearing," Stafford explained to me. "It's nature's way of helping her get along with Polly."

Hap chuckled at this left-handed reference to the ear-splitting quality of his wife's voice.

A wiry man with a slight limp rose from the bench down from Stafford and me, and at a signal from Hap, approached us. Hap said, "Tom, I'd like you to know Laidlaw Utley. I introduced you to him when we first came in, but if you're like I am, it will take a spell for all the new names to sink in, and for you to connect the names with the faces. Utley is the best bronc rider I've ever seen. I was privileged long ago to see you, Tom, when you used to be a fair-to-middling bronc rider, on the day when you rode a horse that one and all said couldn't be rode. It was the time you rode a wild one the boys called Banjo out at Sam Clarke's place. And I'll say this, you rode him to a standstill; you rode him to a fare-thee-well. Many a man who was there said we'd never see the likes of that ride again. Well," he expanded, clearly proud of his man, "that was before I seen Laidlaw Utley at work. I swear, if you could get a saddle cinched up on a cyclone, Utley could ride it."

The bronc rider looked extremely embarrassed at becoming the object of our attention. He shook his head and said it wasn't true, and that he'd never known or heard of a man who'd been thrown as often as he had. "If I'm such a good rider, how come I've had so many broken bones? How come I have to walk around with a gimpy leg?"

The conversation turned to the wild horses, and all of the men told stories of the power and the speed of the black stallion which Thatcher and I had seen.

I turned to Laidlaw Utley and asked him, "If we caught him, do you think he could be broken to the saddle?"

He hesitated a moment. Then he said that he doubted it, that a horse like that would kill himself and anyone trying to ride him, and that it would be foolhardy to try. He added, "My opinion on the subject don't matter much, for there ain't a chance in hell of catching him. You can't get within a half mile of any of those wild horses."

Hap's ranch, with its three natural divisions—Basin, Valley, and Mountain—had been further divided into workable areas that could be covered in a day's ride. While the ranch had around twenty-two sections of land, or twenty-two square miles, if you like to think of it that way, this didn't count the unusable parts, such as the high mountain peaks and the rocky and wooded slopes that were of little use for livestock. I was told by Hap that his entire place covered more or less fifty sections, but he had not had it surveyed. It struck me that such a survey would cost a good bit, and with or without it, the land would support the same amount of stock.

Hap was explaining all of this to me as we rode out. The sun's first rays glanced off the remarkable white peaks of the snow-capped mountains to the north, the direction we were headed. Hap said, "In about two weeks we can cover the entire ranch, and check out most of the stock. By then it's time to start all over." The men this day were working the Mountain division, and on reaching this high country, we separated into three groups. Stafford Darnell took two men and went west, Laidlaw Utley took Hap's boy, Jeff, and the other two cowboys and rode to the north of them a ways, while Hap Cunningham rode east of the others with Thatcher and me along to keep him company.

We came to a narrow trail that rose from the rich grass that grew at the foot of steeply ascending mountains, and we rode toward a gap which formed the pass into the rangeland on the other side that Hap had told me about.

Thatcher Stone had been very quiet ever since we had arrived the day before, but now as we rode along together, he spoke with feeling to me. I could tell that he was as impressed by the mountains and trees as I was. In spite of being in the midst of them for some time, neither of us had become accustomed to such beauty. Come to think of it, I don't know if anyone ever becomes completely used to beauty. In all its different guises it somehow retains the capacity to cause surprise and awe.

Thatcher, without changing his tone of voice—although he completely changed the subject—began to fuss. He said to me, "A man could ride himself to death in this country." He complained for a bit more, saying he wished he had learned to be a gambler or somebody who lived indoors.

"You'd die of boredom," I answered dryly. Then I said, "A minute ago you acted like you were having the time of your life. Now you're unhappy. What happened to change things for you?"

"I got to listening to myself," he admitted. "I sounded like a kid."

I laughed. "No more so than me."

Then he startled me. He said, "I'm going back to Black Horse tomorrow."

"You think that's wise?"

"Of course it ain't wise. Wisdom don't have anything to do with it," Thatcher replied.

"Then why take the chance of getting killed? J. K. Cade will know if you come to town."

"I don't think so. You see," he argued, "I'll sneak in when it's dark."

"Why on earth would you do such a fool thing as that?"

"Damn it," Thatcher Stone fumed, "I've got to go see Emma Lake. I been thinking about her ever since we got run out of town. I'll slip in and see her, and then slip back out."

I saw there was no way to talk him out of his plan. Some things in nature are most predictable. Iron filings will invariably snap onto a strong magnet. A pretty girl has much the same effect on a twenty-year-old man.

I was thinking these thoughts when we came to a broad, level place in the trail. Off to the right lay a peculiar box canyon. The opening to it couldn't have been more than fifty yards wide, but it opened up a short way back until it widened to perhaps a quarter of a mile across, and it extended between sheer rock walls for half a mile or so. At the far end of it I saw movement, and I pulled up on my reins.

I rode Joe, and his ears perked forward—he saw what I did. The wild horses could be made out grazing in a flat at the end of the canyon near a stand of evergreen trees.

I hollered at Hap and Thatcher, who had ridden ahead of me. They turned, wondering, and I raised my arm toward the canyon's end. At that instant the big black stallion turned toward us, head high, looking defiant. Then he reared straight up, pawing at the air, and I heard the alarm his whinny gave. He held himself erect before a white boulder, and a shaft of sunlight fell upon him. Then he dropped back and began a cautious lope around the mares to get them started toward us. He lagged back at first and then seemed to change his mind. The stallion's lope changed to a run and then he was charging past the mares, headed straight at us, with a hundred followers behind him.

"Quick," Hap bellered, unlimbering his rope. I saw Thatcher grab for his, and I reached down to untie my own. Hap spurred his horse toward the opening of the box canyon, shouting back at us, "Forget the other horses—let's get three loops on that black stud. They're going to have to come right past us."

The stallion now seemed to be flying as he gathered speed. We had moved to one side of the opening, and our horses were jumping ever' whichaway, and nickering at each other.

"Good God," Thatcher said, "have you ever seen such a sight in all your life?"

CHAPTER EIGHT

The mares thundering toward us in a nervous-looking gallop flattened their ears back as they neared the narrow passage where all three of us crowded to the sheer rock wall on one side to give them room to pass. The big black stallion raced through their midst as if he'd been shot out of a cannon, and we found ourselves facing a stampede. The mares switched from their gallop into a frantic run, trying to keep up with the black which flew to the front, and then there was no way to hold our horses.

We were pulling their heads almost into our laps, hauling back on the reins with our left hands, and unlimbering our ropes with our free right hands. We had already made sure the ropes were secured to our saddle horns. I saw Thatcher having trouble with his mount, and as the mares boomed past, I saw Ross rear up before he jumped forward in pursuit, but by this time I had my own problems, for Joe like to have run clean out from under me. Out of the corner of my eye I could see Hap grabbing at his saddle horn for balance, and all of us were leaning forward; the one thing every cowboy thinks about at a time like this is not to fall under those flying hooves.

The whole pack of us exploded out of the box canyon down the trail that led east through the pass toward the other side of the mountains. Hap and I rode on the left side of the mares by this time, but Ross had carried Thatcher out in front of the stampede, right behind the swift black stallion.

"*Son of a bitch*," Hap hollered, "look at that red roan go!" And in all truth I'll confess to amazement as I watched Ross seem to fly as he and the black stallion crashed over bushes and rocks, and careened downhill out of the pass. Thatcher had about as much control over Ross as if he had his saddle on a log being thrown by white water over a high waterfall.

Thatcher stood in his stirrups, leaned forward as he twirled his loop, then threw it out—flat and hard—around the black stud's head. It slid down where the neck swells out with muscle, and strained back over his shoulder. The mares crashed by them as the snared black wheeled to the wide-open valley to his right, with Thatcher hauling back on Ross, who hadn't been trained yet for roping. By then Hap and I made our way through the wild herd of horses, trying to get close enough to help. I guess I raced a hundred yards ahead of Hap by this time, gaining fast. Joe, my horse, was almost as fleet as Ross.

An incredible thing happened about this time. There was a tall dark juniper tree standing in the way of the black stallion's charge down the rock-strewn slope, and he raced squarely for it, heading just to the tree's left side. At the moment that he reached it, he bolted right. Ross, running behind him, ducked his head and jerked to the tree's left, with Thatcher holding on for dear life. The two big stallions, linked by a tough lariat rope which went from the saddle on Ross to the black stallion's neck, hit the barrier. It looked like both horses had been struck by steam locomotives going the other way, for the rope popped into the thick juniper tree between them—and something had to give. The wild black and Ross must each have weighed in at fifteen hundred pounds or more, and for a quick flash, they both snapped back—completely off their feet. The rope held, the girth didn't, and as it broke, Thatcher rode a saddle through the empty air while Ross turned a complete somersault. The black snapped around as the impact jerked him down. He tumbled over, then rolled to his feet, jumped up, and bolted off. The rope around his neck yanked the saddle and its broken cinch—with Thatcher still hung up in it.

I'll say this for Thatcher. He stayed with that saddle as long as he could, although I'm pretty sure he was tangled up with it and didn't choose to make the ride that followed. First the wild stud jerked him and the saddle into the juniper tree. Thatcher bounced about ten feet off to one side, hit the hard dirt, and caromed about four feet in the air on the end of the rope as the terrified stud flew through the rough country. But then the crazed wild horse shot through a stand of pines, and I lost sight of them.

When I arrived, Thatcher Stone wasn't dead. He raised up on the ground to a sitting position and pulled some green branches from around his neck. He checked to see if anything was broken, and due to his youth and good condition—and probably to a miracle—nothing was. Thatcher spit out a mouthful of dirt and pine needles and blood. His shirt and britches were damn near ripped off, and he had cuts and scratches and scrapes from one end to the other. Blood streaked down his face as he looked dumbly up at me. My mount, breathing hard, moved around nervously.

"Whose idea was it to rope that horse?" Thatcher finally was able to ask.

We found what was left of Thatcher's saddle in the crotch of a tree a half mile away. The badly punished rope hadn't come loose from the saddle horn, but had broken near the loop. I felt grateful in a strange way that the big black stallion had fought free and hadn't been killed. It struck me that if the cinch on Thatcher's saddle hadn't broken, things could have been a lot worse. It probably would have broken the black stud's neck, and God knows what might have happened to Ross and to Thatcher.

I dismounted and examined the frayed ends of the rope. Then Hap joined me in studying the situation. We hunkered down on our bootheels for a spell. Hap asked if I seriously wanted to catch that wild horse and try to ride him. I informed Hap that I took my responsibilities as a husband and father too seriously for such a thing. He got to laughing then, and for a while we talked about the sight of Thatcher holding on to the saddle at the end of a rope as it bounded off trees, rocks, and hard dirt.

Finally we wiped the tears from our eyes, and set out looking for Ross. The red roan was cut up, sore, and bruised, but otherwise all right. However, he had developed a terrible temper, and it took us a long time to catch him. While we were doing that, we came across Thatcher's hat with the fancy band around it. Then we spent an hour fixing Thatcher's saddle as best we could, and getting it on Ross. Finally the three of us headed for the pass on the way back to the Cunningham ranch.

We rode in silence most of the way, though Hap snickered every now and then. "Where in hell *were* you two?" Thatcher finally demanded. "I thought all three of us were going to rope him," he kept saying. Hap and I couldn't help it. We howled with laughter, but Thatcher saw no humor in the situation.

At nightfall we got back to the ranch headquarters. Thatcher heated water, put it in a tub, then crawled in, boots and rags and all, without taking the time to undress. "Don't hardly seem worth the trouble," he apologized. "I was almost buck nekkid anyway."

"You getting ready to go see your gal friend?" I asked the forlorn, battered cowboy as he slumped in the steaming water.

"No," Thatcher Stone replied, "I reckon I've had all the fun that I can stand."

CHAPTER NINE

A good many things happened in the next two weeks. Santiago and our four Mexican cowboys showed up with their remuda of four cow ponies each, which comes to twenty head, plus six to make up the three teams for the chuck wagon. More important, they brought the fifteen thoroughbred brood mares, and all arrived in very good condition. Old Chato, whose real name is Xavier Sanchez, drove the chuck wagon.

Most of Hap's cowboys had never seen a thoroughbred before, and they were impressed. This breed of horse looks as though it must have extra bones in its back, for it's so stretched out. They have a delicate-looking head, sensitive eyes, and carry themselves with grace and pride on long, slender legs. Everyone knows about their speed, but seeing it at first hand is a different matter altogether from having an understanding about it.

After a few days of rest the thoroughbreds got real playful, especially on cold mornings, and it was very difficult to keep them on a range where they could be found. I got worried about that wild black stallion running off with them, and Hap and I spent a good bit of time trying to figure out a solution. We finally decided to fence the box canyon up in the Mountain division of the ranch, and keep them there. Since we had no wire, we made a tall fence from cedar and small pine trees. Prisoners in state penitentiaries breaking rocks have approached their task with greater pleasure than our cowboys did when we dug out two double-bit and three single-bit axes, and rode out with the chuck wagon for what was not going to be more than a two-day job. I don't recall hearing so much cussin' in all my life.

After that, Hap Cunningham and I went to Black Horse to meet with Clyde Phillips at the Cattleman's Bank. He had me sign the papers which would get $135,000 transferred from my savings account in the Fort Worth National Bank to Hap's account in Black Horse. Phillips didn't say much about my use of the name Tom Germany in Montana and Tom English in Texas, but he did agree not to mention it, fixing me with a long, curious stare from behind his gold-rimmed spectacles. The ability to raise this amount, taken together with the $10,000 I'd already deposited, got his attention. In a time when cowboys earned a dollar a day—and spent it—not many men could lay their hands on that much cold cash.

Hap rolled a cigarette with fingers turned yellow from holding too many short cigarettes for too many years. After lighting up, he held the limp cigarette in his mouth while he talked, squinting all the while through blue, curling smoke. "Clyde, I made Tom the damnedest offer you have ever heard of. I told him I'd sell him an undivided half interest in the HC spread—lock, stock, and barrel—for a hundred and fifty thousand dollars."

The banker looked at him as though about to ask a question, but Hap kept talking. He said, "I know you think that's too damned cheap, and it is. But then Tom got to telling me how hard up he is, and how he's going to put his fine horses into the deal, although later on he reneged and held out those two studs he rode up here; and what with one thing and another I accepted his counterproposal of a hundred and thirty-five thousand just to shut him up." He beamed at Clyde Phillips and at me, and I could tell he was well satisfied with the deal. Like most folks, he had started out with an "asking price" that he'd have been thunderstruck to get.

"This is far and away the most money in actual cash I've ever had," Hap admitted.

The banker got a lawyer to draw up the papers for Hap and me to sign, which we did after we had lunch at the Elk Antler's Hotel. The banker swore the lawyer to secrecy, and on the contract I noticed that he identified me as "Tom English, a.k.a. Tom Germany, hereinafter to be referred to as 'Germany.' "

The lawyer, a bony, older, tired-looking man named Hugh Witherspoon, told me that "a.k.a." meant "also known as." He said to me, "I've heard of you, Mr. English." He looked at me as though he expected me to do something wild, and both he and the banker appeared to be uncomfortable in my presence. It occurred to me that they had been talking about my past.

"It's important to me that no man know that I'm in Montana," I said to Hugh Witherspoon. "I've never broken any laws, but I've had a few problems. That's why I'm here. I plan to live a peaceful life as a rancher."

The lawyer and Clyde Phillips assured me that I should rest easy; that they would never betray my presence to a living soul.

Folks tend to tell a man to "rest easy," to "relax and not worry," when it is clear as a bell that he can't do any of these things. If a man is able "to relax" whenever he wants, not a soul will ever be caught telling him to do so. Only people who *can't* relax are instructed that they ought to take it easy. I had good reason for feeling nervous. Hap and his wife, Polly, as well as Stafford Darnell and his wife, Thelma, knew me. Now it seemed that I'd given myself away to Clyde Phillips and Hugh Witherspoon. Then, there were Santiago and Chato and the four Lazy E cowboys who all knew me well. With all these people aware of my identity I had no hopes of remaining anonymous for long. But I figured that if I laid low in the mountains, I could still start my new life as I'd planned.

If I could have come out here and cowboyed for someone, I'd have been able to keep my secret. Or I could have lived on my income. But, dammit, the excitement in my life is working out situations where I can watch things grow. That's what I like about ranching as opposed to investments. Instead of sitting at a desk looking at figures on a piece of paper, you get to deal with land, you get to ride out on it in the clean, fresh air. You work with growing grass, and calves and colts. It sounds so simple, but I find it to be more fascinating than I can tell you. The chart which Hap showed me, with a target for a herd of 21,000 cattle in three more years, made me feel like a kid at the prospect of getting the first horse of his very own. The fact that we'd face difficulties added spice to the prospect. Solving problems can be exhilarating. But the whole game plan could get blown from Hoolay to Chunk if some raw, would-be gunfighter got wind of the fact that Tom English was ranching in Montana.

Hap and I sat at a table in Buffalo Ed Schoonover's saloon together with Georgia Wichita. Georgia brought out a bottle of her private stock, which turned out to be a rich, amber-colored bourbon. "Here's to your new partnership," Georgia said, holding her glass up in a toast. After we drank to it, she said, "Hap, the girls and I haven't seen you for a *month*. Where on earth have you been keeping yourself?"

Hap turned a few shades of red, and avoided looking at me. "Been right busy," he mumbled, then took a drink to cover his confusion.

A dark-haired girl came over and sat on his lap. "How you been, darlin'?" she inquired.

A rumble of laughter came up out of Hap's belly, and he said to me, "No real harm for an old dog to go out and hunt every now and then, I don't reckon." He gave the girl a slap on the rump and said he'd been mighty fine, and that after a spell they'd go upstairs so he could fill her in on all the particulars. Then he told her to go along while he talked, and she left us.

Georgia said, "I got a problem with Emma Lake, Hap. Do you recall the pretty little blonde who has been around here a few months?"

Hap nodded.

"Well," Georgia went on, "she is wearing her feelings on her sleeve for all the world to see. She has fallen for that wild kid, Thatcher Stone, who rode out of here with your new partner."

She turned to me. "J. K. Cade has had his boys looking for Thatcher ever since he shot his nephew. He thought the world of Jodie. J.K. is mean enough in the best of times, but now is the worst of times."

"Is he looking for me too?" I asked her.

"I'm not sure about that," she said. "As I think you know, he considers me to be his woman, but that is not the case." She set her jaw sternly. "But be that as it may, he comes to see me all the time, and when he does, he talks. He has mentioned the fact that you figured in the trouble, and that you and Thatcher Stone left town together. I also heard that some of his men chased you for a ways. But I have the idea that if you stay out of his sight he won't bother you. Just don't get between Thatcher and him."

I drank silently, thinking. Then I asked, "Have you seen Thatcher when he has come to town to see Emma Lake?"

"Well, of course I have," Georgia Wichita replied. "He thinks that he is being so careful that no one will know he's here. But Thatcher wears those big-roweled spurs that you can hear for a hundred yards away. He rides in late at night, throws some gravel up at Emma's window, and she comes downstairs to let him in the backdoor. I stick my head out of my room when they come up the stairs to let them see that I know *everything* that goes on around here." She giggled, perhaps at some memory of the surprised young couple standing before her momentary scrutiny.

Georgia leaned forward over the table, and I averted my eyes from the sight of her low-cut bodice. I have never understood, since half the people on this earth are women, how it can be that the other half should get so easily aroused by the sight of something that with livestock is so understandably functional. Men know perfectly well what women look like and vice versa, but for some reason the fact that women drape a few yards of thin cloth over themselves makes everyone feel that they are as unapproachable as if they had on a suit of steel armor, like in the old days in Europe. Then, when a glimpse of ankle or bosom peeks out, it reminds you that those clothes are not that much protection.

She looked first at Hap and then at me, either unaware of or not caring about her exposed front. I examined the coal oil lamp hanging overhead. Georgia said, "The boy doesn't have any idea of what he's up against. J. K. Cade knows about his coming to town, and he plans to kill him."

I felt the hair rise on the back of my neck all of a sudden. Something more than what she just said bothered me, and the prickling warning got worse. I slid my hand down to get it closer to my gun butt, and then with a small kick of fear realized that I was unarmed.

A big man walked up behind me, and I saw Georgia's face go pale. She jumped up from the table and said, "Howdy, J.K., you know Hap Cunningham, don't you?"

J. K. Cade walked around beside us. "I know him," he said, keeping his eyes on me.

"This here is Tom Germany who is going to be working with Hap at the HC outfit. They're partners as of today."

Cade didn't say anything by way of greetings to Georgia or to Hap. He addressed himself to me. "Your friend, Thatcher Stone, murdered my nephew, Jodie Cade. You helped him get away from his men." He put his hand on an unusual weapon holstered on his leg, a six-gun with a barrel that must have been more than a foot long. The hawgleg reached almost to his knee.

He backed away from the table. Not taking his eyes off me, he ordered, "Georgia—you and Hap get out of the way. I'm going to kill this son of a bitch."

The lively conversation in the saloon, the clinking of glasses, the laughter, and the tinkling of the piano—all came to a dead stop. Then, behind the bar, I saw a man with a heavy, grizzled beard wearing an oily-looking, Indian-style leather shirt with a few tattered fringes on it. He reached down and came up with a heavy Sharps rifle.

"J.K.," the bearded man said, "you know I don't allow no fights in my saloon."

"You stay out of this, Ed."

The saloon keeper said in a hard voice, "You're a good customer, J.K. I'd hate to have to blow your head off." He raised the big-bored rifle with familiarity. You can spot a man who knows his weapon.

J. K. Cade slowly moved his hand away from his gun, and I took a deep breath. For a minute there I'd neglected to breathe. People in the room began to talk in hushed tones, and again we heard the clink of glasses, and the scuffing of chairs. Cade said to me, "I'm going to let you live, stranger. The man I'm after is your friend. You send him in to meet me here in town next Saturday at the stroke of noon."

The people became silent again, and all of them listened to what he said. "I'll be standing in the middle of the street waiting at straight-up noon this coming Saturday, and you be sure your boy is there to face me. If he's too cowardly to come in, my men and I will ride out to find him. We'll do that if we have to burn every bush in Montana and sift the ashes. When we get him, we'll string him up on the highest tree we can find." His eyes shone in a mean way. "Tell him not to try to escape, for I'll have men on every trail looking for him. His only chance to die a decent death will be outside on that street," he said, pointing with one hand. Again he said, "Remember—high noon next Saturday."

Cade looked around at the circle of still faces staring at him. He said, "He will have to pay for shooting my nephew. Jodie was just a kid." Then he turned toward Georgia and said curtly, "I'll see you later on. Meanwhile, you're not to pass time with this man."

Her face flushed with anger, and she snapped, "I'll choose who I drink with."

If looks could kill, she and I would both be dead. But the big man walked out the door, and I saw the bartender put his rifle down.

Hap asked, "Are you going to tell Thatcher to face Cade?"

I hesitated a moment. "I'm going to tell him to get the hell out of Montana. There ain't no way for Cade's men to watch all the trails. But if he insists on staying, he'll have a better chance man to man against J. K. Cade than he would later going up against him as well as those gunslingers who ride for him."

"Your friend Thatcher is left with a hard choice," Hap commented. He drained his glass of whiskey, then he and the lively girl who'd spoken to him earlier sauntered off, leaving us.

I asked Georgia to tell me exactly what had happened in each of the previous fights Cade had been involved in, hoping I could learn something that might be useful to Thatcher. She told me the stories, and patiently answered my questions.

Georgia and I drank silently for a time. "You're worried, aren't you?" she asked, and I agreed that I surely was. She put her hand on my arm in a familiar way and looked deep into my eyes. I found this to be pleasant on the one hand, and damned embarrassing on the other.

Out of the clear blue sky she said in a husky voice, "Did I tell you before that I think you're mighty good-looking?"

I cleared my throat. "I'm mighty married," I finally replied.

"I know," she sighed, sliding her chair closer, so her arm touched mine. The room had become overly warm, it seemed to me. I loosened my collar, and she began to laugh. "Being married don't seem to bother all men the way it does you." She nodded at the stairs where Hap, his arm around the dark-haired girl, was vigorously climbing.

In the next hour I drank more than is customary for me, and when I rose to walk out in the street for a breath of air, the room seemed to tilt a little. Later I went back in and sat by Georgia Wichita again. She said, "It is so seldom that a man appeals to me. I'd almost forgotten what it feels like." She managed a small smile, then said, "Don't pay any attention to me." Later she remarked, "I sure wish I'd found you first."

Hap came down the stairs alone, looking foolish, and said it was time we got ourselves over to the hotel, since we'd need to leave early the next morning for the ranch. He said, "You know, we deserved this celebration, partner."

I grinned and agreed that we did indeed. But Georgia wasn't smiling. She said to me as I rose to leave, "J.K. is going to kill your young friend. It won't even be a contest." She closed her eyes, and I noticed again how pretty she was. "It makes me sick at heart," she said. "When it happens, don't try for revenge. I don't want anything happening to you."

CHAPTER TEN

"I'll fight him," Thatcher Stone declared, jumping to his feet. "That's fine with me." He began to stride back and forth in the bunkhouse. The rest of the men were outside tossing steel washers at a hole in the ground, a game that they enjoyed playing. Some of them were pretty good at it.

"I'll take on J. K. Cade *tonight*," Thatcher said.

"No. He said he'll meet you at the stroke of noon on Saturday in the street out in front of Schoonover's saloon."

"That's six days from now. I don't feel like waiting around. If you're going to get it on with a man, well—hell—why wait around?"

Thatcher came back to his bunk and slumped down on it. I sat on one across from him.

"You could go back to Texas," I said, repeating what I'd advised him to do earlier.

Thatcher got up again, walked over to the wall where his gun belt hung from a nail, and took his six-gun out of its holster. He stuck it out toward the cookstove in the middle of the room, closed one eye while he aimed, and said, "Kapow." Then he put the gun down and said, "This J. K. Cade is pretty well known. After I take him, I expect people will talk about me. Probably the newspapers will write stories about Thatcher Stone."

He began to chuckle, full of nervous energy, and he bounced up, put the Colt in its scabbard, returned to the bed, and flopped down on his back. He tilted his hat over his eyes, and crossed his feet, one boot on top of the other. "I'll tell folks that I'm known as 'the Montana Kid.' " He jerked to a sitting position. "That sounds pretty good. What do you think about it?"

"Thatcher," I replied, "if you won't take my advice about going back home, then I think you better let me work with you, so you'll be prepared for Saturday. I had a close friend who was a gunfighter, and I used to help him practice."

"Who was this friend?" Thatcher inquired.

"Jason Field," I said.

"I never heard of him," Thatcher commented.

I'd only told half a lie in saying that I'd watched Jason Field practice. The old gunfighter—turned rancher—had hired me when I was a kid. When I got in trouble, he worked long and hard showing me how to clear my six-gun in a hurry, and how to use it when it got down to killing or being killed. He had taught me all he knew about the gunslinger's craft, which was considerable.

The next day the cowboys rode off with Hap; and Thatcher and I walked our horses to a ravine a few miles from the ranch headquarters. We stepped down from our saddles, and tied our reins securely to tree branches. Then we went a few hundred yards down the draw to a good place where there was no chance of a stray bullet hitting any livestock.

Thatcher looked uncomfortable when I told him to think of the cedar tree ten feet away as a gunslinger throwing down on him. He slapped leather clumsily, and his .44 bullet whanged off through the branches. He grabbed his pistol with both hands, and on the third shot nicked the tree trunk, his target.

"You sure you don't want to go back to Texas?" I asked.

He glowered at me, and I could see he wasn't playing a game. My question had made him mad as a hornet.

"You think you can do better? God damn it, do you?"

I told him to cool down, that we had all week to smooth things out. He insisted that I shoot at the tree, taking off his gun belt and handing it to me.

I told him I'd go through the things slowly that I'd been talking about, so he could see them. After buckling on Thatcher's rig, I hefted his Colt. The balance seemed off a mite, but somehow it felt good in my hand, as if it belonged there.

Thatcher's face had a strange look on it as he watched me. I put it down to nerves, for he wouldn't be normal if he weren't afraid.

"Always tie the scabbard to your leg. That's why I punched a hole in the bottom of it this morning and put these tie-down thongs in it," I said to him, demonstrating. "Then, when you take your stance, bend your legs a little—like this. That cants the six-gun to the rear, and makes it stick out just a bit away from you, so when you make your move"—I stopped speaking and slowly drew it out—"you'll find the gun butt in your hand. As it clears the holster, bring it up, but not high. Keep your forearm close to your hipbone for support. I want you to learn to hip-fire; don't ever bring it up to shoulder level like you did a minute ago. You don't have time for that." Then I told him, "Point your pistol as you'd point your finger. I want you to draw and hip-fire in one smooth motion. Work on smoothness, and after a time, the speed will come."

I turned to the tree to show him what I meant. "Keep the tension out of your hand and arm—keep it from your shoulders. If you get tense, you'll have jerky moves. And *don't* grip the Colt too tight. That's real important. Think about keeping a light grip—but a firm one."

Thatcher watched, fascinated, and sweat beaded on his forehead. I felt so damn sorry for the kid I didn't know what to do. It occurred to me that I had only once had a definite time set when I would have to face a man. All but one of my fights had somehow happened suddenly. I'd never had to wait except that one time, and I knew how anxiousness could eat away at a man's insides. The occasion I had known in advance of an unavoidable gunfight waiting for me happened when I faced the man in black who had sent word for me to face him. But he had killed my closest friend, Culley Clarke, and the rage I'd felt had cleared out much of the fear.

"Show me," Thatcher said, his voice little more than a whisper.

I faced the tree, loosening the Colt in its holster. Then I bent my legs slightly and let things happen. The six-gun seemed to fly into my hand—and as it did three bullets crashed out, and shock waves from the swift explosions set off echoes. Birds which had landed moments before in the top of the tree shrilled and chattered, wheeling into the sky.

Thatcher walked up and stared dumbly at the three splintered holes in a tight triangle, each about an inch or two from the other, in the center of the rough-barked cedar tree.

"God almighty," he said, awestruck. "How on earth did you *do* that?" Then he said, "I thought you said you used to watch a *friend* practice."

Son of a bitch, I thought to myself. Why did I have to do that? After being so careful about concealing my identity, I had come perilously close to giving myself away to this kid. I'd seen the way he liked to brag. If he had any idea who I was, he'd tell the world.

"Thatcher, I'm *slow,*" I said. "I wouldn't think of getting in a gunfight. Why do you think I don't wear six-guns?"

"That was slow?" he asked in hushed tones.

"Of course it was," I said. "I don't want you to even think about trying to become a gunfighter. I've seen a few, and they have something they're born with." I paused before I stated the obvious. "You are *not* a born gunfighter."

I had shaken the hell out of him. He asked, "Are you telling me that what I saw you do wasn't fast?" His face colored. "Dammit, Tom, you're trying to scare me and I don't appreciate it. If something happens before my eyes so quickly that I can't even *see* it, don't try to tell me that it was *slow.*"

I backtracked a little. "A quick move here or there is just part of it, Thatcher. When you face a person who has a gun on you, something happens to almost any man's nerves. His brain doesn't work just right. His muscles tend to freeze up."

Thatcher didn't say anything. I added, "I saw you when Jodie Cade forced your hand. You didn't want to shoot him, but when it was obvious that you'd have to—you hesitated."

His eyes grew angry. I said, "Thatcher, I don't say this in any way as a criticism. In fact, it's just the opposite. You are a decent human being, and I admire you for it. Good folks have been taught from birth that they must not kill. It's one of the ten commandments."

Then the cowboy acted odd. "I don't want to hear about such things," he said. He picked up the gun belt I had taken off, and strapped it on, cussing and fuming, as though trying to build up his nerve. Once he had the Colt on, he drew it out, practicing with it hip-high, but not firing. He said, "People will hear about Thatcher Stone. They are going to know about the Montana Kid."

"That is plain crazy," I started to say, but he cut me short.

He said, "I ain't going to run off to Texas, and J. K. Cade ain't going to kill me. I'm going to kill him. You helping me or not?"

"I'll help," I said reluctantly.

Thatcher set to work in earnest. Fortunately we had a good supply of cartridges, for he burned a fair amount of gunpowder. After a while he turned to me and asked, "Is Cade one of those who is real fast with a gun?"

"I'm not sure about that," I replied, "but I don't think so. I talked to Georgia Wichita about the five men he has killed, and he always seemed to be where he had an advantage. From what I heard he tends to be tricky. But, to answer your question, in no case did he make a fast draw to down anyone."

Thatcher held both arms out, stretching. He took off his hat with his right hand and wiped his brow with his left sleeve. Then he sat down on a log in the shade. I joined him there, and told him what I'd learned from Georgia.

She began with the story about Jim Wichita, her husband. Cade had paid Georgia attention when she came to town. She explained that she worked in Buffalo Ed Schoonover's saloon back then, and said that maybe that gave Cade the idea that he could treat her any way he pleased. She worked since her husband was a drunkard and couldn't keep body and soul together without her help. One day Jim Wichita sat drinking while she laughed and talked to J. K. Cade. Wichita stumbled over, grabbed Georgia by the hair, and slapped her around a good bit. Then he went outside on the street. Georgia told me that she had heard the rest of the story from other people, for she went back to work. J. K. Cade followed her abusive husband outside. He pulled an axe handle from a barrel in front of the hardware store, and began battering Jim Wichita on the head. He managed to get up and stumble off into an alley, the one down the street next to the Gold Miners' Bar. No one picked him up or looked at him. People don't pay much attention to known drunks, Georgia had explained with some bitterness. She said that she no longer loved her husband, but she was used to him. When he didn't come to the saloon as he normally did at nightfall, Georgia went out to find him. When she did, he was dead.

"What about the others?" Thatcher asked.

"Georgia told me that a gambler and Cade had words over the way the cards were being dealt. The gambler, a regular hard case of a man, pulled a derringer, but Cade told him he wasn't armed, but that he had a gun on his saddle. He told the man to meet him outside. When the gambler walked out of the saloon door, Cade stood behind his horse with a ten-gauge shotgun balanced on his saddle. He like to of blown the poor bastard in two."

Thatcher looked upset. He fidgeted around and picked at the bark on the log.

"In the other cases," I continued, "J.K. shot a drifter he accused of changing a brand on one of his steers. It happened on Cade's ranch, and only his own men witnessed the shooting. All they said was that they considered it a fair fight, which I doubt. Then there was the time he had his pistol out under the poker table when a man told him to draw. The poor devil had no more than said that when he took a forty-five slug in the belly."

Now Thatcher looked as though he were very upset. He busied himself, rising and practicing his draw a few times, more or less doing it now the way I'd shown him.

"Last year," I said, "J. K. Cade took that ten-gauge shotgun after a miner who pulled a knife on him in an argument that broke out over a woman. Cade killed him, of course, and claimed he shot in self-defense. No one felt like arguing with a man who had a reputation like his, so that was the end of the matter."

Thatcher held his forearm firmly against his side, pointing the gun barrel at the tree. He squeezed off a shot that missed. Then two more that knocked hunks of dusty cedar bark flying. "Hey! Did you see that?" Thatcher called out, turning to me, his white teeth shining as he grinned.

Then he turned gloomy again. "I wisht it was Sunday," Thatcher said. "When Sunday comes, I'll be with my gal, Emma, and all the folks will be warning their friends to stand clear of that mean sonuvabitch they call the Montana Kid."

CHAPTER ELEVEN

Santiago and I spent Thursday beyond the pass on the other side of the mountains. We saddled up around four in the morning, so by midday we reached a place I'd run across the week before. I sat there for a time, completely caught up by the sight. Tall trees—western larch, aspen, and Engelmann spruce—stood on the grassy slope, and they moved in the cool summer wind of Montana. I stepped down off Midget, a fat bay mare with the smoothest trot I've ever ridden. Santiago joined me. We looked at the river curling a hundred yards below, and I said, "This is the site I've been telling you about. What do you think?"

"Don't see how you can beat it," he replied.

Santiago spoke English with a pronounced accent, the way most Mexicans in our part of Texas do, but he spoke it well. His father, Benito, and I had stood side by side in the showdown at Three Points years before near the Concho River, and he had been my salvation in the small, bitter range war that followed it. While it might not have compared with the Lincoln County Wars in New Mexico, for those of us caught up in it, matters were serious enough.

In my mind's eye I could see a ranch house for my family—for Sally and Rebecca. I walked around, feeling a little clumsy on foot, with my bootheels catching on the tall clumps of grass. A sweet smell, a lot like honeysuckle, swept around me, and I saw wild flowers growing nearby. Some of them were the kind called bitterroot that Polly had pointed out to me. Santiago and I talked about where we'd put the house, the barn, the bunkhouse, and corrals. We paced things off, and made big plans. As the conversation kind of wandered in and out, I sensed the excitement that grew in him. With all my failings I have one gift that has served me well: I can motivate the men who work with me to try to help make things work out.

We rode back through the pass, then took down some logs at the entrance to the box canyon, and went in to check on our mares. After leading our horses through, we put the logs back up behind us.

"I'll bring the boys out here next week. We'll build a real gate," Santiago said as we rode along, looking for the thoroughbreds. "We'll have to use leather for hinges." A thought struck him. "Try to find some hinges or a blacksmith who can make some for us when you get to Black Horse."

I jumped a little at the thought of going there, although I knew I had no choice in the matter.

"You can't face that trouble without your guns, Tom. You never know what might happen," Santiago said, as though he could read my mind.

"I left them back home. It's best for me to go unarmed."

"Your wife worried about your leaving them. When we rode out on our way here, she brought them to me. They're in a box in our chuck wagon at the ranch."

An electric tingle struck the pit of my stomach and spread from there. "Well, I'll be damned," I said. "She's scared for me to wear them, and scared if I don't."

We went down a swale, and as we started back up, I saw a big yellow cat stalking, gliding slowly along a high slope at the edge of the canyon wall. I pulled my Winchester from its saddle boot and spurred Midget. She scampered hard, but I missed the bounding speed I would have had with Joe or Ross. When I got to the rise, the mountain lion had disappeared in the boulders.

"I'm worried about our mares," I said to Santiago when he clattered up beside me, reining in to a sliding stop.

"You needn't be," he said, and I turned to him, wondering what he meant. He pointed down the canyon toward the little creek that meandered at the end of it. "They've got protection," Santiago said.

I looked with amazement at the big black stallion we had chased a few weeks before, as he stood with his head held high —between us and the mares. "Lord have mercy!" I hollered, although not because I'm especially religious. Some expressions that I must have heard my grandmother use pop out of me when I least expect it—usually when something takes me by surprise. Then I yelled at Santiago, "There must be another way into this canyon."

At that moment the stallion leaned into a high lope that turned into a run. He was on the other side of the canyon from us, maybe three hundred yards away, as he swept past, and the fifteen thoroughbred mares matched him stride for stride.

Santiago, whipping his pinto with his reins as if they were a quirt and spurring hard, burst through the brush after them. I followed right behind. But putting the spurs to Midget couldn't give her longer legs.

The trespassing stud and our mares flared ahead of us. As they approached the seven-foot-high log and brush fence, the stallion slowed—and I figured he'd pull up or circle. But then his muscles bunched as he surged forward even more swiftly than before, and gathering himself, he lunged up and out—and soared like a strange black eagle, like a streak of dark paint splashed against the canvas made by the clear blue of the sky— and by God made it! His hind feet just hit the top log and it rolled down on the other side.

"*Madre de Dios,*" Santiago howled, and I figured he had the same problem I did.

The stallion pulled up on a crest above us, half reared and whinnied, then he bounded away.

The mares turned in tumbled confusion, and swirled back in a swift crescent—heads tossing, manes and tails flying—as they wheeled away from the fence in a panic. I never heard as much neighing and nickering horse talk. Even my fat little mare began fluttering wind through her nostrils between the times she whinnied back at them.

Finally the mares settled down. Then, as though nothing had

happened, they began to crunch on the tall grass, jaws grinding methodically. A horse will eat all day if he can. He'll even eat while you're riding him if you don't keep his head up. Even then he'll grab at leaves as you ride by a tree. But I suppose if I weighed twelve or thirteen hundred pounds, I'd have to eat a good bit to keep my strength up.

"We'll have to add to the height of this fence," Santiago observed, as the two of us grunted and strained, putting the displaced log back up where it had been. We had already closed our makeshift gate, and I felt an urge to get back to ranch headquarters.

"Let's leave the fence as it is," I said. "It's high enough to keep our stock in, and I'm tickled to death for that wild stud to come pay his respects. He'll make one hell of a sire. We've got plenty of time to put Joe and Ross with the brood mares later. We're going to be looking for a good crop of colts every year from now on. But I'll tell you what we might think about doing, we might add to the height of the fence with him inside. Then we could have a chance at rounding up those wild mustangs in his herd. There must be a good hundred of them, and some looked like good horses to me."

"How many of our mares do you reckon he topped?" Santiago wondered out loud.

"Hard to say. But he'll be back. And he knows all about mountain lions and wolves and bears. He'll help us take care of our stock until we can move up here so as to keep a better eye on things. And if we're lucky, we might be able to catch him someday."

"Don't look at me when you hunt for someone to break him," Santiago said. *"Madre de Dios!* Whoever heard of a horse jumping a seven-foot fence? If a man should ever be able to climb on his back, I would expect that big black to get real excited, and then God only knows how high he'd jump."

There is nothing as good for your appetite as being half starved. Luther Hawkins, Hap Cunningham's crusty old cook, fair beamed with pleasure as I kept helping myself to more of his rock-hard sourdough biscuits, semi-cooked frijole beans, and burned steak. Then, feeling like a human again, I strolled outside to find Thatcher Stone. The cowboys, as usual, were hard at their game of throwing washers at a little hole in the ground, and even though the bets they made were small, you'd never have guessed it to hear the agonized groans of the losers or the war whoops of the winners.

I found Thatcher standing by the shed next to the corral, with its smell of horses and sweat and leather. Inside the shed some saddles hung by mecate rope loops tied to their horns. Others rode on two-by-four boards that formed a half-wall dividing the shed into two rooms. Saddles, saddle blankets, bridles, and extra equipment, like surcingles, extra girths and cinch rings and the like, filled one room. The other had oats in bins, and things like curry combs, together with bottles full of dark purple and brown medicine for livestock. We walked inside the shed to get out of the wind. I took down a rope, threw it on the floor except for the end I held, and began to re-coil it.

"You spend the day practicing with your forty-four?" I asked Thatcher.

"If I don't know how to pull a trigger by now, it's too late to learn," Thatcher snapped, his nerves obviously on edge. He spun toward me. "You don't know how hard this waiting is. I haven't slept in two nights and . . ." His voice broke off, and he turned away from me.

"It ain't too late to back away," I told him gently. "None would hold it against you. J. K. Cade is known far and wide for fighting mean and unfair. You'd be walking alone into his town —knowing that he may have backup men around him. I've told you what has happened before. He's never faced anyone unless the cards were stacked in his favor."

"He can't do that this time," Thatcher said. "He threw down his challenge in front of the whole town. They'll all be there to watch. He'd never get away with using a backshooter or such-like on Saturday." The certainty dwindled out of his voice and turned into doubt. Weakly he looked at me and asked, "Would he?"

"I don't have any idea of what he has in mind, Thatcher, but you can bet your bottom dollar that he has a plan that he considers a lead-pipe cinch. My hunch is this. He'll go into the street wearing that custom-made six-gun I told you about, and it's my bet that he'll be carrying his double-barrel ten-gauge shotgun. Now, he would know that the average cowpuncher is not going to walk up too close to a man holding a scattergun. He'd figure you might stand off—maybe about fifty to seventy yards away. That's when he'd drag out that long-barreled Colt. I wouldn't be surprised if it had that range. It has to be more accurate than most handguns, although it is not made for a quick-draw fight."

Thatcher snorted. "Nobody can hit the broad side of a barn at the distance you're talking about." In spite of the certainty of his words, his voice showed his concern.

"Maybe not. I never heard of a gunfighter depending on the accuracy of a handgun except up close. In nearly every case they get nearby, maybe ten or fifteen feet away, but rarely farther than that. However, if Cade has a rifleman hidden out to help him, a thirty-thirty or a forty-four-forty bullet could take you down in the confusion without much chance of bystanders noticing where it came from. They'd see J. K. Cade rattling off one shot after another with his long pistol, and they'd see you go down. In a case like that, eyewitnesses see what their mind tells them they ought to be seeing."

Thatcher asked, "What can I do, Tom?"

"We'll have to give you some help to make sure it's a fair fight. Or as fair as we can make it."

Then we talked some more. I told him we'd have our own men all over the place to head off any attempt made by a hidden rifleman. Then I said that Cade would expect him to ride in from the north. I suggested that he start off by doing something unexpected to take Cade off his balance a little, by circling around and coming into town from the south. I told him to get there a little early so he wouldn't feel rushed; then to get down and loosen up, get the kinks out, and try to relax. I explained that it doesn't do to rush at a time like this, that the most important thing is to have a cool head.

"It must be real nice telling someone else just how he should act when he goes out to get shot at," Thatcher complained. "If I live through this, I'll make it a practice to advise other folks in the future."

"It's more comfortable," I agreed. Then I told him that I had talked to Santiago about what to do. I explained that Santiago and the four men from the Lazy E weren't strangers to trouble. They wore guns and could use them. They were to be fanned out on both sides of the street to look out for interference.

"So the long and short of it," Thatcher said, "is that I'm going to be free to walk down the main street against a man carrying a ten-gauge shotgun and a long-range handgun. I've got to thank you, Tom, for this help. By God, it's good for a man to know he's got friends." He'd been leaning against the shed's wall, but he moved from it in exasperation.

I put my hand on his shoulder to try to calm him down. It's funny how fond I'd gotten of the kid in the short time I'd known him. Again I said we ought to call the whole thing off, but he refused. I got the impression from the things he said that he had bragged some to his gal friend, to Emma Lake, and he'd rather run the risk of a bullet in his gut than look bad in her eyes.

I sighed. "If you're bound and determined to go through with this thing, then here's what I'd suggest."

He began to scoff, asking how come I figured on helping him out of a situation that neither I nor any man had ever lived through. But I came up with a lame excuse, saying that my old friend Jason Field had told me a fair amount about such things. "If you'll quiet down, I'll tell you how to save your hide if you're interested," I insisted.

Thatcher crawled up on the half-wall that divided the shed and lit the lamp that hung from the ceiling. It came in handy, for many a time cowboys had to work on their gear at night—or find it before light in the morning. Then, like a damn fool kid he sat on a saddle that straddled the wall, with both feet in the stirrups. "I'm listening," he said.

"See that you do," I barked at him. "This is a serious matter."

Thatcher Stone tipped his hat back, and crooked one knee over the saddle horn, waiting for me to stop fuming and go on with my counseling.

"Thatcher, I want you to wear your Colt and carry that Model Seventy-three Winchester you're so proud of. Then, when you approach Cade, stand off about a hundred yards away, and make a sudden move. Try to make him jump and throw down on you. To my way of thinking he wouldn't have a Chinaman's chance of hitting you with a bullet or with buckshot at that distance. But when he makes his move, take him down with your rifle."

"That would be murder," Thatcher said in a hushed way.

"That would be killing a man bent on killing you. It would be using his own plan against him. You'd be doing to him what he figured on doing to you, except you'd have taken his tactics a step further."

"What would people say?"

"Thatcher, what the hell difference does that make? You'd be alive. You wouldn't have fired the first shot. They don't have any Marquis of Queensberry rules in gunfights."

"Any what?"

I ignored the question. "Forget it, this here is a different thing altogether."

Thatcher said in a reflective way, "No matter how I get him, I'll be known as the man who gunned down J. K. Cade." His eyes got fierce. "By God, I can't hardly wait until it's Saturday, when I have that son of a bitch in my gun sights!"

CHAPTER TWELVE

Not a damn thing worked out the way I figured it would. It's enough to make a man give up on making plans altogether.

I prepared to leave for Black Horse on Friday, a day early, after Santiago pulled my guns out of their box in the chuck wagon. I stood there, faced with the choice of whether to put them on and run the risk of falling back into my old way of life—or to walk away without them. I was tired of feeling weak and vulnerable, so the decision didn't take but a split second. My God but they felt good! For the first time in a long while I had their protection again.

I unwrapped them with loving care, then buckled the gun belt which had its loops filled with .45 cartridges. The two smooth scabbards were soft from the neat's-foot oil I'd rubbed on them. I fastened both holsters to my legs with their tie-down thongs, and slid the precisely matched pair of Colts in them.

Before leaving, I rode off to the draw that lay about a half mile from the barn on Joe, tied him, and went to a sheltered place to limber up. I worked on pace and timing, letting things happen; first the right gun, then the left, then both at once, creating a ricocheting drumbeat of a cannonade. After an hour I went back to the bunkhouse where I took the two finely balanced six-guns apart. With great care I cleaned and oiled them. Some of the HC cowboys had heard the racket, and they came inside to find out what I had been doing, but I guess they saw I didn't feel like talking. None of them said anything to me. By now they knew my true identity, I guess. It's hard to keep cowboys from talking, and they'd been getting friendly on a gradual basis with my men from Texas.

I guess I'm slow on the uptake. All of a sudden I realized that
if the others had found out about me, then Thatcher must have
too. It struck me as odd that he hadn't commented on it, for I
had never noticed Thatcher going out of his way to be diplo-
matic in the past. But maybe he had changed. I decided that
maybe I'd been hasty in judging Thatcher Stone. The trouble at
hand had matured him, it seemed to me.

That afternoon late I got to Black Horse. After putting Joe up
at the livery stable, I walked over to the hotel, carrying my Colt
.45s wrapped in my bedroll, and with my rifle stuck under one
arm. A man in the lobby stared at me with great intensity while
I registered. He looked to be in his forties, and his nose had fine
red veins at the surface, a condition some say is caused by too
much whiskey and high living. He wore a thick-knotted bow tie
that hung lopsided. Many men put those things around their
necks every day as a matter of course, but I've never had one on
in all my life. They serve no decorative purpose. I've yet to see a
man look better because he has latched a cloth hackamore
around his head.

When I turned around, he still had his eyes fixed on me, and
he didn't look away.

"Do we know each other?" I asked.

"We haven't met," the man answered, rising from the cane-
bottomed chair. He held a bowler hat and wore a dark suit.
Staring at me from behind steel-rimmed glasses, he walked up
and held out his hand. "My name is George Lindstrom," he
announced, "from Chicago."

"Tom Germany," I said shortly. It makes me uneasy when
strangers try to strike up a conversation for no reason.

"You're a long way from home," he commented in a flat voice.

I looked at him coldly. That was a peculiar thing to say. "No,"
I said. "I'm not but one day's ride from my ranch."

Who *is* this man? I wondered about it, then decided, the hell
with him. But the name rang a bell. Where had I heard it? I
shrugged it off, and went upstairs to drop my gear on the bed.

I had decided to come in a day early to see for myself that J. K.

Cade and his men didn't do something to catch us off guard.
Later I entered Buffalo Ed Schoonover's saloon. Ed came over
to my table with a bottle and a glass.

"I never had a chance to thank you," I said to him, "for
pulling that big buffalo gun out from behind the bar when J. K.
Cade took after me. I'd have been in one hell of a spot without
you."

His voice rumbled out, as though from the bottom of a well. "I
run a peaceable saloon, and I'll shoot the butt off anyone who
gets violent in here."

I hid a smile. "I admire any man who'll kill to avoid violence,
especially when it's aimed at me."

Then I asked, "Will Cade stand and fight fair against my
friend tomorrow?"

"He don't know the meanin' of the word," the grizzled old
buffalo hunter said, stalking back to his place behind the bar.

Georgia Wichita came down the stairs with what looked to
me to be a brand-new dress. I complimented her on it, and she
flushed with pleasure.

She sat beside me and said, "I saw you ride into town, so I
decided to wear it. I ordered this dress out of a catalog almost six
months ago and it just got here. Do you think it fits all right?"

"Georgia, you know good and well that you had to use a
shoehorn to slide into that dress. I don't know if you can breathe
or not, but it surely does look fine." I spoke the truth. Most
women's clothes out here are built for comfort, and keep the
sun and wind off. But the dresses this woman wore would make
a statue take notice. The shiny material matched the startling
dark blue of her eyes. I examined her face, not for the first time,
noting the fullness of her lips, her short straight nose, and high
cheekbones.

"Why are you staring at me?"

I laughed. "Guess it's been so long since I've been around a
pretty woman that I'd forgotten what one looks like."

Most people enjoy compliments, and Georgia was no exception. "That's the nicest thing I've heard since I don't know when," she said.

Then she got serious. "J.K. is up to something, but I don't know what it is."

I poured her a drink, and refilled my glass.

"He's been in town twice with his men this week, but he hasn't dropped by to see me. Reckon he's mad about my taking up with you."

I must have looked puzzled, for she burst out laughing and explained, "I told him you were my boyfriend, and you asked me not to take paying customers anymore, even old friends like him." She sounded bitter when she said the word "friends," making sure I didn't think she considered him to be one.

"What caused you to say a thing like that?"

"I don't know. It just popped out." She looked at me from the corners of her eyes through thick, long, curling lashes. "Maybe it was just wishful thinking. But the fact is, I'm making good money managing the girls' business, and Ed gives me a cut on the whiskey money we help him earn. I have free room and board, and not too many expenses except for my clothes. So I figured now is as good a time as any to get 'respectable' again."

I smiled, but stopped when I saw the unexpected hurt look in her eyes. I said, "Well, Georgia, I'm proud of you," and she looked pleased as punch.

"What do you suppose Cade and his men were doing in town?" I asked.

"I have no idea, but they spent some time with Jelly Biggs."

"Jelly?"

She giggled. "He got that name long ago due to the fact that he has a big belly that jiggles when he walks. Jelly has been the sheriff for the last six months, but he used to work for J.K., and some say he still does."

"Can he be depended on to see that no one tries to backshoot Thatcher?"

"I can't answer that," Georgia said. "But everybody in the whole town has been discussing the showdown for the last week. Seems like they can't talk about anything else. With as many people out watching as there are bound to be, surely nothing like that will happen."

I didn't answer. From what I'd heard of Cade, I wouldn't put anything past him.

"I know you're here to look out for any meanness J.K. may have planned. My room upstairs overlooks the street out front, and it's about as good a place as you'll find to keep an eye on things."

She held out her hand to me. "Why don't you let me show it to you right now?"

The heat rose up in my face. I didn't know what to say. I'd been away from home a long time, and all of a sudden a good many not unpleasant sensations ran through me.

When I didn't answer, Georgia said, her voice trembling, "Don't guess I've ever been turned down before. I'm surprised how bad it hurts."

Her big blue eyes filled with tears, and she hurried away to my considerable relief. If she had stayed about one minute longer, my good intentions might have crumbled.

Saturday morning dawned clear. A rooster out behind the Elk Antler's Hotel strained his throat greeting the day, apparently bound and determined that every hen on the mountain should hear him. He crowed with considerable energy, over and over, as though he figured the sun wouldn't make it up in the east without his help. I opened my eyes—wide awake on the instant. The knowledge of danger slid like a thin knife right into the pit of my stomach.

By ten o'clock Santiago and our four Lazy E cowboys showed up looking prepared to fight the battle of Shiloh single-handed. If they'd carried any more guns, their horses wouldn't have made it to town. I met them and we talked. All of us were coming close to that reckless state where everything seems to be in sharper focus.

I paced up and down the main street, carrying my Winchester, feeling the heavy potential of the two Colts strapped to both legs. George Lindstrom, the man I'd seen the day before in the hotel, had pulled a chair out on the sidewalk across from Schoonover's, and he sat there, tipped back against the wall of the hardware store, his bowler hat square on his head shading his eyes.

I saw no sign of J. K. Cade or any of his gunmen. Standing before Buffalo Ed Schoonover's saloon, I spoke to Santiago briefly. Two of our cowboys were stationed on either side of the street to the north, and two were in similar positions to the south.

Santiago pulled a steel-cased railroad watch from his pocket. "It's half past eleven. Where do you think Thatcher is?"

"Probably circling around to the south of town. We thought J.K. would arrive early. It would be one hell of a note if Thatcher rode into Cade and his men by mistake," I said.

Santiago walked swiftly to his horse, which he'd hitched on a side street, and rode off to scout the situation and head off Thatcher if necessary.

Feeling jumpy, I stepped into Schoonover's saloon. I waited for my eyes to adjust, standing in the cool, darkened room, smelling the reek of stale beer and spilled whiskey. A bar can be a lively place at night, with sparkling lights and laughter and people. But in the mornings a bar is hollow and haunted. It's filled with a sad and ugly emptiness—with a lonely silence, not to mention a terrible odor.

Georgia Wichita came down the stairs, and in a moment stood beside me. "I couldn't sleep last night," she said. "I feel like such a fool—throwing myself at you. And I'm sick at heart at the thought of your young friend having to face J. K. Cade this morning. He must be terrified—I know *I* would be."

She stood close, and I smelled a trace of perfume and soap and clean hair. I looked down into her wide, worried, deep-blue eyes.

"I do believe you've shrunk," I said.

She laughed quickly. "I forgot my shoes; I'm barefooted." She grinned in an impish way. "I hate to wear shoes." Then she became serious. "There's not much time. Do you want to see my room? As I told you, it overlooks the street."

I nodded.

"Quick," she said, "follow me. It's fifteen minutes until twelve. There's not much time."

The five girls who at night sported green, red, and yellow satin dresses sat in plain cotton kimonos, their young faces washed clean of rouge and paint—making them look like kids. They kept getting up and running to the front to look out to see if the fight was getting ready to start. The anticipation of excitement swirled through the room. The girls smiled and whispered to each other behind their hands when Georgia and I walked upstairs. One of them laughed out loud in a brassy way. I felt my cheeks turn hot with embarrassment.

"Don't mind them," Georgia said with amusement. She opened her door, and I followed her inside. It was a larger room than I had expected, and as neat as a pin.

She took my hand and led me beyond the bed to the heavily curtained windows. "Let me help you," she said, pulling them to one side.

I would later think about those words. "Let me help you," she had said.

I looked out, and my heart almost stopped. Across the street, looking right into my eyes out of an open second-story window, leaned the man with the dirty brown hat who worked for J. K. Cade. He held a rifle in his hands, and he jerked back, wheeling toward me.

I started to cry out to warn Georgia, but then the crash of shattered window glass came at the same time that I heard the rifle's sharp report. A second shot ripped wood from the window casing and I felt splinters sting my face.

I dropped down low, both guns out, and began to rise, when Georgia slumped against me without a sound. She spun off, hit the floor, and lay there. For an unbelieving, blood-frozen instant I stared down into her dark blue sightless eyes. Then I saw the bright wetness pumping from her chest. The first bullet had struck her squarely; it must have killed her instantly.

The minutes ticked away. I'd holstered my six-guns, and rested now on one knee. I called out her name, and had my hand beneath her head. Inside a voice kept saying: you've seen these things before, get hold of yourself. But I couldn't seem to move. Then the silent paralysis of shock wore off. Hot tears sprang unbidden to my eyes, and I rubbed them angrily with my shirt sleeve. An electricity built and spun within me.

I closed Georgia Wichita's eyes with great gentleness, and saw my fingers tremble. Moving back to the wall away from the window, I took out my guns one at a time, checked them, and slid them back in their holsters. My Winchester stood propped at the wall by the door where I'd put it on entering the room. I'd come back for it later.

Feeling cold as ice or colder, I went swiftly down the stairs and out the backdoor of the saloon. I came around the corner moments later, and shouldered through the drawn-back crowd of thrill seekers.

Out in the street I saw the man in his brown hat, and the ugly bald giant, and J. K. Cade—standing before the Gold Miners' Bar. Cade had his shotgun as I'd thought he would. They were talking urgently, and as I stepped closer, they saw me and moved apart.

I fixed my eyes on the bastard in the brown hat. I wanted to get at him. The bald-headed man, the one whose brow bulged out—who looked like a white, hairless gorilla with an underslung jaw—pulled his pistol out, and held it down by his side. It appeared that he planned to get even with me for the time I flattened his nose with my knee.

I spied Santiago and two of our boys. Thatcher Stone was nowhere in sight. The noisy crowd grew silent—as though one and all had stopped breathing. There must have been more than a hundred of them, and they drew back out of the way as I moved to the center of the street to face the three men. From the corners of my eyes I saw the onlookers standing with their mouths half open—hungry for blood and death—the kind of people who go out to watch public hangings.

A deep, dark hatred welled up in me. J. K. Cade stood responsible for Georgia Wichita's death, regardless of who pulled the trigger.

The three men fidgeted a little. J.K. pulled back both hammers on his shotgun, but held it pointed down, a little off to one side. The man who'd shot at me and killed Georgia dropped his rifle onto the rutted, dried mud of the street and fastened his hand on his pistol's butt. The ugly brute with the bald head swung his pistol back and forth with his long arm. He had vacant-looking eyes, and stared at me as if he didn't have a care in the world.

I stopped about thirty feet away from the three men. I held both hands out from my sides and called out, *"Cade!"*

Things happened fast. But at times like this your mind races faster than events, and in spite of the quick rush and flow of them, you see things clearly. The three men lunged together, but my six-guns were firing in less than the blink of an eye, both exploding at the same time. I took the brown-hatted cowboy in the chest, though missing off to one side a little. The bald man ducked, and the shot I'd meant for his body exploded his forehead. J.K.'s shotgun bellered out while still pointed at the ground, as two bullets hit his belly and a third caught him in the center of his breastbone. The brown-hatted man rolled over and pushed his gun at me, but I shot him twice, and he shuddered for the last time.

The echoes of the pistol shots rolled up the narrow street. I stood with both guns out—trembling from head to foot. The smell of gunpowder filled the air. I looked around quick to see if anyone held a gun on me, but saw only Santiago and his men with weapons. They had jumped out on the street and had their revolvers out as they backed toward me.

I guess that when people who aren't present when these things happen hear of them, all they learn is that a man went down. In a newspaper it's almost like boxers fighting, for you don't read about any terror or screaming or pain. The only blood is like something in a painting, a color around the quiet, unfeeling body of the loser in the game. That's the big problem. Folks think of these terrible events as being contests.

Automatically I holstered my left gun, flipped the cylinder of the right one open, and reloaded. Then I did the same with the other Colt. Off to one side I saw Thatcher Stone on foot, walking cautiously down the street, with his .44 in its scabbard, but his Winchester held in both hands. The crowd of people began to shout and cry out to one another, but they still hung back.

A man appeared above us on the wooden sidewalk which stood on the high side of the slanted street, so it seemed as though he looked down from a platform. I saw the person who had introduced himself to me as George Lindstrom the day before at the Elk Antler's Hotel. He braced himself rigidly against a post and announced to all who stood within earshot, "Gentlemen, you have just seen none other than the legendary Tom English of Texas, the fastest gun in the West. You can tell your grandchildren about this day. You've seen a piece of history before your very eyes."

Men and women straggled forward from both sides of the street, skirting the scene of slaughter, but staring at it with morbid fascination. They waited in a semicircle beneath the man who had spoken to them. His voice issued forth again, loud as an orator making a speech on the Fourth of July. "I've been writing about Tom English for the *Chicago Weekly* for a long time. I have searched for him high and low for months, and have followed his long trail from Texas to Montana where I find him using the name of Tom Germany."

The writer stared down at me, and it was then that I knew where I'd heard of him. I remembered the magazine article with his name on it which Hap Cunningham had shown me, the one which had my engraved picture. I've always heard that writers are peculiar people. This one truly bewildered me, for he acted as if I was—in some odd way—his own particular invention.

The people drew away from me as though I were some kind of pariah. A dreadful fear and horror seemed to run through them, and I knew how I must look, standing with two tied-down six-guns directly beside three bloody bodies lying in the torn dirt of the street.

Thatcher Stone, pale as a ghost, walked up to me. He said, "I was making a wide circle around the town like you told me to, and I got lost. I arrived just as you faced them." His lips quivered just a little, and he clearly found it hard to speak.

"I've never seen anything like what you did. You didn't seem to have a chance." His voice choked up, and in a whisper he added, "There were three of them. They'd have killed me." He looked sick.

George Lindstrom held his hand out stiffly and pointed his finger at me. He said in a strangely triumphant way, "I have written about this man—and there were some who didn't believe me. But now the entire town of Black Horse, Montana, stands witness that *Tom English is the most dangerous man alive.*"

CHAPTER THIRTEEN

Sheriff Jelly Biggs and two deputies escorted me to his office, a small room in front of the town jail. Santiago and his boys gathered outside, talking quietly in Spanish to each other. I saw Santiago carrying my rifle as well as his own, which raised a question in my mind.

The deputies looked nervously out the window at my men, and then at each other. Few Mexicans lived in Montana, and I had seen that many considered them to be a mysterious and scary people. Under the present circumstances I welcomed this attitude.

The sheriff's imposing belly swelled out like a woman who is near her time, and he had a dewlap under his chin that would have made a Hereford bull proud.

Jelly stuck out both his hands and said to me, "I'll take those guns." His two deputies flinched and backed against the wall.

"No, sheriff," I said, pulling out a chair and sitting down, "you won't."

He stood stock-still for a minute, then backed off and took a chair behind his desk. The deputies relaxed.

About then Hap Cunningham strode in, breathing hard. "Is Jelly charging you with anything, Tom?"

"No, he's not, Hap. He has a job to do is all. He has to sort things out." Then I said, "I didn't know you'd be in town."

"I had to come, Tom. Didn't want to be the only man in Montana to miss the showdown." He wagged his head from side to side, and a corner of his mouth tucked in for a minute. "It sure as hell worked out different than I would have figured."

"Such things usually do," I responded. Then I said, "I guess you heard about Georgia."

A sick look crossed Hap's face. "It fair breaks my heart, Tom."

The sheriff looked as unhappy as an old dog, his coat full of burrs and dirt, who is being dragged toward a trough for his once-a-year bath. "It don't seem *possible* that someone as full of life as Georgia could be gone—that we won't never see her no more." He drew out a red bandanna from his back pocket and blew his nose as if it was a trumpet.

He put his bandanna away and fussed with papers on his desk. The two deputies and Hap and I waited. Outside a wagon pulled to a stop. Men gathered up the still figures of the dead and placed them in it. Then it drove off.

Sheriff Jelly Biggs said, "All of us heard two shots and the sound of glass breaking. Landon and Winford here," he jerked his hand toward the deputies, "went into Schoonover's to see what happened, and found Georgia lying there. They came across your rifle."

The man named Winford said, "I gave your Winchester to that Meskin who works for you."

"It would be best for our town, Mr. English, if you'd go back to Texas," Jelly Biggs husked.

"Are you fixin' to run me out?" The cold anger I felt found its way into the sound of my words.

"You've broken no laws, but . . ." He began again, "We see enough trouble around here without the country's best-known gunslinger settling in with us."

Hap broke into the conversation, saying heatedly, "Jelly, damn your bones, this here is my partner. I need his help. We're going to be working hard at the ranch." He lowered his voice from a holler to something more like a bellow. "I don't appreciate what you just said."

Finally the sheriff sighed and looked at me. "Mr. English, if you'd give me your side of the story about what happened, I'd appreciate it."

I told him without wasting many words about the day's

events. He asked a few questions, and then struggled out of his chair. He came around his desk and approached me.

"J. K. Cade scared the bejeezus out of me," the sheriff said. "It's true I worked for him once, and he helped get me elected. But I never felt safe or comfortable around the man." Then he commented on how much everyone had cared for Georgia Wichita, and as he did, he choked up. His shirt stretched tight over his formidable belly, and it quivered mightily.

"We'll miss her," Jelly Biggs said at last. Then, in a firm way, he added, "Now that I've had time to think about it, I guess you done a good thing for our town. You won't need to worry none about the rest of Cade's men coming after you. I know each and every one of them, and without Cade and Pooley and Toad, they'll drift off. They're like a bunch of dogs that are brave in a pack, but not much by theirselves."

This was how I learned the names of the other two men I shot. I listened to the deputies who began visiting quietly off to one side with each other, and gathered that Pooley wore the dirty brown hat, and the people in town gave the ugly, bald-headed cowboy the nickname of Toad, though probably they didn't say it to his face.

Hap said, "Funny thing about J. K. Cade is that he had a brother who was as different from him as daylight from dark. Lewis Cade is a fine man. He and his wife, Sara Ann, had given up on Jodie, that wild kid of theirs who Thatcher Stone shot. Jodie was a sore trial to his ma and pa." Hap stopped to think before he went on. "And there wasn't no way that Lewis could handle his brother J.K. I'll talk to Lewis if you'd like me to, Jelly, but I can't see him or anyone else for that matter looking for revenge. It ain't as though J.K. was the kind of man to attract friends."

Hap stared fixedly at the sheriff. "Jelly, as you may know, Lewis Cade is a good cowman, and he mainly wants to look after the ranch he and J.K. were building up. He was telling me not long ago that he'd do well if he could keep the damn rustlers off his range." He glowered at the rotund lawman. "Are you fixing to do something about Bull Doggett and that gang of his? He's stealing us blind."

"You've got no proof of that, Hap," the sheriff said defensively.

"I'll get the proof," Hap said, swelling up. "I'll ride there and look over his herd to see if I don't find cattle wearing my brand."

"Doggett keeps armed men in the pass that goes to his place," Jelly Biggs stressed, while Hap stormed back at him. With both of them talking at the same time, I couldn't catch the sense of what they were saying, although it struck me that they were not in agreement. I walked out of the sheriff's office while they wrangled.

I've been involved in more than my share of gunplay, but the older I get the less I seem able to bear the aftereffects. I hesitated in front of Schoonover's saloon, but I couldn't make myself go in there.

Santiago stood beside me on the board sidewalk. "Get a bottle," I said to him, "then bring it to me at the livery stable." The importance of finding a place without people overwhelmed me. I ignored a hundred stares and walked deliberately away from the center of town.

When Santiago arrived, he found me flopped down on a feed sack behind the stables. I leaned back against the wall, shaded by the overhanging roof. Beyond me in the corral a few poor-looking horses stretched out their necks and looked at me. Even the horses were staring. I half closed my eyes as I uncorked the bottle with a pocketknife. Santiago sensed I didn't want company, and he walked away.

The raw whiskey drunk straight from the bottle stung and scratched its way down and hit bottom as if I'd swallowed a mouthful of red-hot coals. My face twisted up and I coughed and spluttered, waiting for the pain to pass by. People do the damnedest things in the name of fun.

By the fourth or fifth pull from the bottle's neck I had pretty well killed out the nerves in mouth, throat, and belly, and a strong warmth spread through me. The only good thing I can say about liquor is that it does have a way of making the time pass. And if you drink enough, you're supposed to be able to wash away your memories. I clutched the brown bottle the way a little, frightened kid will his mother's skirt. A tingling gradually spread to my face, and my head began to reel. I put one hand down on the dry dirt to steady the world. With both eyes held wide open, and a hand firmly planted, I was finally able to get the earth to settle down from its swaying.

Santiago came back to see how I was doing. He hunkered down beside me, and after waiting a time, he began to speak. For some reason an odd ringing filled my ears and I had to concentrate with all my might to make out what he said.

"I heard two rifle shots, but couldn't see anything. I moved out to look, and then the man named Pooley came out of the building across from Schoonover's and went up to Cade. About the same time the big one called Toad ran out of the dry goods store across the way. They must have been there all morning getting set to take Thatcher if Cade looked like he needed help. But, anyway, just as the three of them got together, you walked out."

Santiago didn't say anything else. Neither of us wanted to talk about the bloodshed.

"What about Thatcher? Where is he now?" I asked.

"You didn't see what happened?"

I shook my head.

"Right after the shoot-out, as you left with the sheriff, a young girl with long blond hair came running down the street and grabbed him around the neck. She was crying and laughing at the same time, and Thatcher couldn't pry her arms off. Finally he did, and the two of them went into Schoonover's saloon. I haven't seen him since."

"That would be Emma Lake." I told Santiago what little I knew about her, including the fact that Thatcher Stone thought she hung the moon.

Hap Cunningham walked from the back of the stable and

found us behind it. "Well, *here* you are. I been looking all over for you. What in tarnation are you doing?"

By now I'd lost what little common sense I've got. "Howdy, Hap," I greeted him. "Haven't you ever felt like sitting on a feed sack?"

He looked disgusted. "Let's get your things and head for the ranch."

"What about Georgia's funeral?" I asked.

"There's too much excitement and commotion in this town for me," Hap said. "Georgia would understand—in fact, you know damn well she'd want you out of Black Horse."

I got to my feet awkwardly, confused about the difficulty I had in standing upright. "My legs have gone to sleep, I do believe," I apologized, as Hap supported me.

"More like your brain, it looks like to me," he answered.

I had to tell him something that at the time seemed important. The whiskey must have affected my tongue. It had certainly taken the life out of it. I spoke with considerable care. "The last thing Georgia said was 'Let me help you.' "

"What did he say?" Hap asked Santiago.

Santiago answered, "I couldn't make it out—something about Georgia."

Hap said, "Give me a hand. Let's get him out of here. That goddamn reporter is trying to find him, and Tom is in no shape to give an interview."

CHAPTER FOURTEEN

We had to spend the night in town, but left before daylight the next morning. None of us spoke for the first few hours. People have died feeling better than I did. If any other man had done to me what I had done to myself, I would have had every reason to call the law out on him. It stands to reason that, since the time many centuries ago when man first discovered alcohol, there had to be one hangover that would stand alone as the daddy of them all. I took no pride in having it. When I could think of anything except my blinding headache, I realized I had a thirst that went beyond description.

We came to a narrow river. Before crossing it, I dismounted deliberately and knelt with care before falling down on my stomach to put my face into the coldness. Upstream from me my horse stuck his nose down and began to drink in jolting uphill ripples. As horses often do, he pawed with one forefoot in the stream before he began. I paid no attention to the muddy water.

Hap said, "For God's sake, Tom, get on the other side of your horse."

"It don't matter," I replied, "I'm going to drink it all anyways."

For the rest of the day Hap repeated that to himself as though I had been joking when I said it.

Thatcher Stone rode out to the ranch to see me two days later.

He stepped off Ross, and when I came up, he apologized for

the lather on the horse. "Didn't mean to ride him so hard, Tom."

"Where have you been?" I demanded. "We've been damn concerned about you."

"I had a hard time getting away from Emma," he apologized.

In spite of his rough trip he looked good, and wore a new black broadcloth shirt that matched the color of his curl-brimmed hat. The afternoon sun glinted off the gold coins on the hat's crown.

After supper Thatcher asked to talk to me alone. "I've had the offer of a job in town," he said.

This put me back on my heels. I had more or less taken it for granted that he'd stay with us, and had looked forward to it.

"You going to clerk in the hardware store?" I asked.

"No," he answered indignantly. "Jelly Biggs' two deputies quit. They said they'd never been around gunplay until a few days ago, and they didn't want any part of it."

"You mean to say he hired *you* as a deputy?" I asked, unable to disguise my disbelief.

"He sure did. He saw me in the gunfighter rig you fixed for me—and of course he knows I'm a friend of yours." He looked at me for a long, silent moment, as though he saw me suddenly in a different light. Almost shyly he added, "I told the sheriff we rode together, and how you worked with me on gun handling and such." For a moment he looked embarrassed, but then he continued. "Anyway—the sheriff said that anyone who could ride into Black Horse to face J. K. Cade alone had a fair amount of nerve, and he said he wanted to hire a man as his deputy who had some starch to him."

I said nothing about that. I didn't ask him why he had been late for his showdown with Cade, or anything about his claim about getting lost when he circled the town.

Thatcher beamed with pleasure as he pulled his denim jacket to one side. "Look here," he said, proud as a kid with a new toy. "I got a badge."

Sure enough, there on his chest a dull tin star hung limply.

"You're going to get tired of town life," I remarked.

"I'll work on getting used to it," Thatcher replied. "The cold is coming on, so I plan to be where I can put my boots up right by Sheriff Biggs' stove all winter."

"How's Emma?" I asked.

He colored. "She couldn't be better." Then he added, "All the girls are real upset about Georgia."

He told me about the funeral, but as he did, I turned to one side. I've never cared for funerals, and have avoided them like the plague. I got lost in my thoughts as Thatcher rattled on about the people at the ceremony.

I had not been in love with Georgia Wichita—far from it—but I did care for her a great deal. There has never been any other woman than Sally for me. I suppose it's all right to have friendships that run deep, though. As so often happens, one thought led into another, and I found myself pondering about Thatcher. It hurt to think he wouldn't be around.

I interrupted his drawn-out narrative, saying, "I sort of thought you might like to work with us here at the ranch. You'd be with us at the start of something that might turn out to be big. The day could come when you might want to think about building up a herd of your own. I'd figured on giving you some help in doing that."

He said he surely did appreciate the kind thought, but without much hesitation he turned me down. He grinned and said that punching cows required considerable work, that a man had to be out with cattle during the coldest days of winter and the hottest of summer, and anyone with any sense at all would avoid a job which made such demands. "Who wants to be dependent his whole life on the weather, besides that?" he demanded. "You either have a drouth and your stock all dies, or you have floods, and your steers get washed down the rivers. I don't believe a man could sit down and study and come up with a more peculiar occupation."

I began to laugh. "Thatcher, you better stop now before you convince me that I'm wasting my life."

The next day before he left I gave him a saddle horse. He had asked for the loan of one so he could get to town, but I told him that the next thing I knew he would be outfoxed by another horse trader, so I might as well supply him with a mount.

The young man stood there, dumbfounded, speechless, and looked at the big buckskin gelding we called Puddle because he seemed to like to go out of his way to splash through them. Tears came to Thatcher's eyes, and having difficulty speaking, he finally said that no one had ever done anything that nice for him before in his whole life. He was so shaken that we had to go back to the bunkhouse for some more coffee before he could leave.

We nursed the mugs of black, bitter liquid which at least had the virtue of being hot, and Thatcher said he had a confession to make. He said, "Tom, I've been meaning to tell you that I was scared out of my skin on Saturday morning when I rode in to face J. K. Cade."

I told him that there was sure no shame in that, for any sensible man would have felt the same. He looked his appreciation at me.

Thatcher added, "I wasn't really lost, as I guess you know. But I sure wasn't in any hurry to get to town." He rose and went to the door where he hesitated, and then walked outside. I joined him. Thatcher kicked at the ground a minute, then looked up. With complete sincerity he said, "You saved my life. I won't forget it."

Thatcher climbed up on his new horse, and by now he was himself again. A great big kid-like grin spread across his face. "How come he's named Puddle?"

I told him and he laughed out loud. "This horse and I are going to get on fine together," he said as he left, hollering back for me to come to Black Horse to see him when I could.

After he left, it occurred to me that not once had he mentioned his feelings on discovering that I was Tom English, the gunfighter. I put it down to his not wanting to embarrass me.

* * *

We spent three months building a snug rock house on the hill beyond the pass, although I didn't plan to move into it until the next summer. I had no intention of passing the winter alone. Hap had published our claim for some 20,000 acres that ran up and down the valley below it, and we'd hired six extra cowboys. In addition we took on a man named Swede Larkins to take charge of the construction. He had a simpleminded helper called Jingle Bob Doolittle who turned out to be an accomplished finish carpenter. He might have been a fool in many ways, but when it came to cabinet work, he stood out head and shoulders above the rest. Once again I reminded myself not to judge a man too quickly. With some of our boys pitching in, they made a good bit of headway on the house, but we still would need to build the barn, bunkhouse, and corral.

The bite of winter swept out of the mountains and for a while I thought I'd get used to it. That was a foolish hope, like getting used to being horsewhipped. Then all of Canada must have froze clear up and shrugged an ice age off on us. It put a stop for a while to everything we tried to do. Snow, the likes of which I've never seen before, began to choke off the passes, and I realized I'd picked a mighty lonesome place to live. The whole bunch of us made our way to Hap Cunningham's headquarters then, while we could still make it.

One thing about it being so cold: the snow fell like fine powder, so it blew and didn't turn into slush or ice. And what that meant down in the Basin was that the wind kept whipping it along so it never got much over six or eight inches deep. The stock could get down to the grass, and with their shaggy winter coats, did fine. But we had to pull strays out of snowbanks and places where they bogged down. We'd head out early every day, bundled up like Eskimos, working with our froze-up ropes with gloved hands to loosen them into reluctant limberness. I wore a heavy sheepskin-lined coat with a tall collar, and had a thick wool scarf I tied over my hat and under my chin to protect my ears. It probably made me look like a Kansas housewife, but that was the least of my worries. I tied a trail driver's bandanna over my nose, so only my eyes and frosted lashes were exposed. With long-handled underwear, cumbersome wool pants and shirt, and fleece-covered chaps—we call them leggins in Texas —you'd think I'd have managed fine. That was not the case. I damn near froze to death.

Each morning we built a fire by the corral in order to warm the bridle bits so the steel wouldn't stick to our horses' mouths. After that we'd head out—with our mounts bucking through drifts up to their bellies. We pulled cows and calves out of the snow, taking them down to the protection of the low parts of the Basin. Hap had predicted that we wouldn't lose much stock, and I hoped he knew what he was talking about. In the meantime, I worried about losing my feet.

When you walk, the circulation keeps going in your feet. But on horseback, with your legs hanging down, the fierceness of the cold causes a pain to set in that passes understanding. Then your feet go numb, and you wonder, when you step down from your horse, if they'll break clear off. When I would finally get back to the stove at the bunkhouse, instead of things getting better, they got worse. The deadness turned back to life in my two helpless feet, but to get there they had to travel right back through the pain that put them in such a fix in the first place. Each time the jagged pain-streaks flickered up from my toes, I let everyone in earshot know what a damned fool I had been to leave the sunswept plains of Texas for the ice-covered mountains of Montana.

My language got so bad that Hap said, "Tom, I'm going to have to see that you spend more time in church, so you'll get out of such bad habits." But I told him there were no churches left in Montana, for surely God had better sense than to winter there.

I no longer worried about the Doggett gang. People are puny enemies when nature itself has turned on you. We made our jokes, but on nights when the blizzard winds howled in the blackness, it was scary as hell. We became well aware of our weakness. Along with all of this was my personal problem. I missed my wife and daughter so bad I could have cried. I even missed the hellish sun and sweat of heat-wave Texas summers. At least a man could go outside at night and take a deep breath without wondering if it would kill him.

Hap and Polly and I usually sat together at night in his living room with the fireplace roaring high, and with the flames spitting sparks when they hit a sap pocket. The smell of the fire, the feel of closed-in warmth and safety, along with a touch or two of fierce bourbon, made things take on a different light. Then we'd laugh about crazy things that had happened that day. No day passed without something to laugh about, and so we kept just on the edge of sanity. Such nights with those old friends kept me from sliding down the other side.

On one of those evenings I asked, "Why didn't you pick out a ranch in flatter country, Hap? You could have settled east of here—a lot closer to Billings or Bozeman. You'd have found it far easier to raise stock there, and the cattle drive to the railroad would have been shorter."

"Folks were already there, Tom. I wanted room. I wanted free range without other men roping my unbranded calves which still trailed their mamas, as though they were mavericks."

"I never heard of a man outside of you trying to raise stock on top of the Rocky Mountains," I said, still complaining.

Hap's beller of a laugh rang out. "I try to work the creases, Tom, and stay clear of the tops of most mountains."

He and Polly liked to tease me. She said, "When you showed up, you kept telling us we'd found paradise itself."

I began to smile along with them. "I don't reckon we'll find a real paradise no matter where we look. There's just too many people around nowadays for that. Come to think of it, as I recall the Bible story, when more than one person arrived on the scene, the Garden of Eden lost much of its charm."

Polly brought me a mug of coffee. "Stop your fussing, Tom. Paradise without people wouldn't mean much. That brings

Sally and Rebecca to mind. Will you go to fetch them when the spring thaw comes?"

"I sure plan to, Polly. To tell you the truth, being without them is driving me crazy."

"I noticed that," she said.

When spring came, it was still winter. But at least the passes had cleared and our men were working on the new house and barn and the rest of it on the East Ranch, as we called the 20,000-acre spread on the other side of the mountains. On Saturday nights the boys working there would leave early to reach the HC headquarters before nightfall. They had shown up late one Saturday toward the end of March, and as usual there was a good bit of horseplay and hoorawin' going on. I sat in the bunkhouse talking to the foreman, Stafford Darnell, and our bronc-buster, Laidlaw Utley.

Laidlaw had just begun a story about the time he tried to get on top of an outlaw called Sidewinder which one and all claimed had never been rode. A half-breed cowboy had one of the horse's ears clamped in his teeth, trying to "ear him down," while another man held firm to the rope around the horse's head. The big bay swung the half-breed around as if he was a rag doll—snapping him against the snubbing post and the corral fence and the ground—to hear Laidlaw tell the story. At last they got the saddle on. There was no way to get that bay to take the bridle's bit, so they settled for a hackamore, and Laidlaw swung up. The cowboy on the rope flicked it off, jerked the bandanna from the horse's eyes, and the half-breed fell, half dead, face down in the dirt. Unbelievably, the horse didn't move a muscle at first, in spite of the tense figure clamped to the saddle upon him. Laidlaw said, "I felt that horse bow up his back like a giant tomcat getting ready for a serious fight, and he began to shake all over. I said to myself, 'Gawd dang, I'm in for it now.' And I was. Instead of bucking, he busted into a high run, jumped the gate, slammed me into a hackberry limb, and we never seen him again. Knocked me clean unconscious. Broke

my left arm, my collarbone, and six ribs." Laidlaw laughed as if
that was the funniest story he ever heard. He rarely smiled
when other folks told tales.

The next morning, being a Sunday, meant we had our usual
lazy breakfast. I generally ate with the men, although I still
stayed up at Hap's house. Just as we finished, I heard Stafford
Darnell call out, and then some other man's voice hollered to us
that we had visitors. Grabbing jackets and hats in the over-
crowded bunkhouse, we straggled outside into the chill, bright
morning to see who on earth could be traveling in this weather.

The sun had broken through the clouds, and the snow glis-
tened as if it had ten million diamonds sprinkled on its surface.
A wagon drawn by four hairy mules crunched on the white
surface, leaving its trail behind. We saw the humped appearance of two people huddled on the front seat under a huge,
frosted buffalo robe. They drew up, and to my everlasting aston-
ishment, I recognized Thatcher Stone, and with him sat Emma
Lake.

The poor girl, bedraggled and half frozen, her hair going
every whichaway, looked as if she had put rouge on the end of
her nose, it was so red. Both Thatcher and Emma had ice on
their eyebrows, and they labored down from the wagon with
their breath making white clouds in front of their faces.

Thatcher said, "Howdy, Tom. Emma and I thought we'd drop
by for a cup of coffee."

Behind him I heard a weak moan and saw Emma half collapse
into Hap's arms. She summoned up the strength to glare, and
said in a quivering, accusing way, "You have tried to kill me,
Thatcher Stone." She turned to face the rest of us and said, "We
been lost in these mountains since day before yesterday." She
looked around wildly, and it struck me she might be looking for
an axe to use on Thatcher.

Nourishment, rest, a bath, and the luxury of fresh clothes do
wonders for the human spirit, and after a time Emma had
agreed not to murder Thatcher, although she stood firm in her
refusal to talk to him again in the near or long-term future. I had

been using Jeff's room, since Hap and Polly's boy preferred the
bunkhouse. But on Emma's arrival, I moved out to the
bunkhouse as well, so she would have a place to stay.

Polly and Thelma, Stafford Darnell's wife, attended Emma,
and coaxed her out of her weeping spells. Downstairs in Polly's
kitchen Hap and I sat with Thatcher and waited for him to tell
us what had happened.

Thatcher said, "All I wanted to do was surprise you all. I had
told Emma about how pretty the ranch is out here, and we were
sick and tired of doing nothing in town, so I got her to agree to
come along. I had thought we'd arrive by Friday night, visit on
Saturday, and then go back to Black Horse on Sunday." He
broke off as the sounds of Emma's wailing in the bedroom
upstairs drifted down to us. "It turned out to be a bad idea," he
said unnecessarily.

In bits and pieces his story came out. They left Black Horse
against everyone's advice in the mule-drawn wagon with picnic
supplies for what they calculated would be a one-day trip. The
rest of the story was one of wandering around looking for trails
that the snow concealed. They spent two nights under the buffalo robe near makeshift fires that Thatcher finally coaxed out of
the wet, cold wood he could find. "When we came to the Basin,
I told Emma I knew where we were, and that we'd make it to
the ranch in a few hours, but by then I'd told her so many lies
she wouldn't believe me." Thatcher accepted a drink of Hap's
bourbon and slumped in his chair, looking woebegone.

Polly and Thelma came downstairs and joined us. Polly
looked at Thatcher coldly. "She wants to talk to you."

Thatcher rose to his feet and started for the stairs, but Polly
brought him up short. "Where do you think you're going? Don't
you dare go into that young lady's bedroom!" With that she sent
him to the living room to wait, and Hap and I went outdoors.

"It appears," I said to Hap, "that your wife doesn't know how
Emma's been earning her livelihood."

"I sure as hell hope she doesn't," he said gruffly. "When
Emma came in the house, she asked me where I'd been for so

long. She said all the gals had missed me." Hap looked glum. "Polly was out of the room and didn't hear what she said, but it was a close call. My wife has put up with my foolishness for a long time, so I don't think she'd throw me out, but she might bang me on the forehead with her iron skillet."

The upshot of all of this confusion was that Hap and I had to ride along as chaperons to look after Emma's virtue when she and Thatcher finally returned to Black Horse two days later. By then Emma had begun to run into the room and flop down on Thatcher's lap whenever he sat down, so it looked as if he was forgiven. Polly considered such behavior scandalous, and probably with good reason figured that without us along Thatcher might take advantage of the situation. We tried to reason with her, but Polly stood firm.

At the time it seemed as though all we had in prospect was a hard trip. I had no idea of what waited for me in Black Horse.

CHAPTER FIFTEEN

About mid-afternoon of the second day the four well-cussed, damn-fool mules hauled the creaking wagon with Emma and Thatcher along the main street of Black Horse. Hap had hitched our packhorse's rope to the wagon, and he and I trailed behind. We stepped down off our saddles at Buffalo Ed Schoonover's saloon to help Emma with her things. She struggled ahead and went up to her room, and Thatcher followed close behind. Curious bystanders stood on both sides of the street to see what in thunder was going on, for the hard winter had kept out most visitors. We learned later that the Concord mud wagons were able to get there on the main trail from the east, but local travelers were few and far between.

Standing inside the saloon for the first time since Georgia Wichita's death, I felt her presence. Strangely, it comforted me, as though some voice said, "It's good you're here. I've missed you." Then sadness struck.

"What's the matter with you, Tom?" Hap Cunningham asked. But he didn't have time to wait for an answer that wouldn't have come anyway, for a lively little dark-haired girl with black eyes grabbed him by the neck, swung her skirted legs up around his waist, and Hap twirled her through the air a time or two with a Texas holler that would have started up the sleepiest herd.

Hap headed for the bar with a gal under each arm, and I arrived at the conclusion that our plan to buy supplies would have to wait a spell. The trip had been hard enough, even though Hap knew of an unused cabin not far off the main trail, so we'd been able to spend the night inside, protected from the wind's cold claws.

I grabbed a bottle and sat alone at a table next to a group of six or seven grubby-looking fellows who had given up on playing cards to be able to devote their full attention to staring at me. "It's him," I heard a man say whose skin looked as though it didn't fit. He had a skull-like look, with hollow places for cheeks, and what little hair he had grew only on the sides and he had plastered it sideways across his head to make it look as though it grew there. Even ugly folks have their vanities.

A gap-toothed man dressed as a gambler said, "By God, you're right. That there is Tom English; I'd recognize him anywhere from them *Chicago Weekly* pictures."

I turned my back and poured a drink while the men behind me settled down, though their talk still buzzed.

At the bar I heard Hap begin to sing a song. Then he ran out of the words he knew, so he switched to teasing the sportin' ladies around him. There are some men who throughout their lives are automatically liked. It can't be their looks or intelligence that causes this, for smarter men than Hap—and those one hell of a lot better-looking—often don't have the gift of attracting friends. Yet here stood Hap, belly hanging over his belt, gray hair sticking out from under his hat, with a smile that wrapped its warmth around the girls, and his love for life seemed to be contagious. It was as though Santa Claus had come to Black Horse on April Fools' Day.

A few chips clattered on the table behind me as the players anted up before the cards were dealt. A few moments later all but three men had folded, and one of them, instead of watching to see the hand played out, came up behind me and cleared his throat.

I looked up and he eased to one side, then pulled out a chair and sat down. He wore a side arm. When I had entered the dark saloon, the thoughts of Georgia had been on my mind, but now the pictures of the things I'd seen registered, and it struck me as odd that all the men were armed. While most folks own weapons, only a few go to the trouble to wear them.

"You people expecting some trouble?" I looked at the bearded man beside me. He would be, I calculated, around forty years old or so. He had thick black eyebrows and a horny, weather-beaten face. I've seen turtle shells that looked softer.

The hairy eyebrows flicked their surprise at me. "You ain't heard about the uprising?" Then he proceeded to tell me with more than sufficient detail about the pack of Indians that had broken from the reservation north of the Missouri, and which had swept down through the snow, slaughtering all whites in their path—men, women, and children. He got caught up in the story, and it struck me that he scared himself with his own tales of rape and torture. "Of *course* we're armed," he said. Then he added, "With them heathen you save the last bullet for yourself. No man should let them savages take him alive."

The others left their gambling to gather around and assure me of the desperate nature of our condition. I told them that the few Indians I had seen were pitiful-looking creatures, half starved to death. But they insisted on their version, saying in effect that a band of painted red men, decked out with feathers and armed to the teeth, were skulking in the woods, bent on scalping every last one of us.

Ed Schoonover lumbered up and said, "That'll be enough of that fool talk." The men, appearing to be slightly embarrassed, returned to their game.

Ed addressed me. "Rumors like this can cause sensible people to panic, and them fellers ain't even sensible. We'd be safer around the redskins than sitting near all these varmints carrying pistols which they don't know how to use. I'll be mightily surprised if one of them don't shoot himself in the foot before the week is up."

He spoke of Georgia Wichita, and I sensed a hidden sensitivity in the rough old buffalo hunter. "She thought you were somebody special," Ed said to me. He respected my silence. We drank together, and I tried to make dark memories and hard-to-explain regrets slip from my mind.

"There probably were some poor, hungry Indians," Ed Schoonover said, returning to that subject, "trying to hunt for food, and my guess is that maybe some of them fought back when white men jumped them. But they ain't fool enough to start no trouble after all that has happened here. Their last hooraw was at Bear's Paw Mountain." Then he commented, "The real problem we've got is with all these damn outlaws. As long as Montana stays a territory, we won't have the law we need. As you well know, the badlands aren't all that far away. Men with bounties on their heads have drifted in from all over, bandits from far and near have come in search of a place to hide out, a place to lick their wounds, where they'll feel safe. It's scoundrels like that which are the threat, not them starvin' red men."

Ed Schoonover said, "You have become a mighty famous man in the last seven or eight months. You was well known before, but it has gone way beyond that now."

He could tell I didn't know what he was talking about.

"I didn't figure you had a chance to see any of them magazines with George Lindstrom's stories, for I knew you hadn't been to town since all the trouble here." He said I'd know about them soon enough, and he had saved all the copies out of curiosity, for to his knowledge their little town had not before been singled out for such widespread publicity. It struck me when he said those words that for him, like most people, even bad publicity beat none at all, but at the time I still didn't have an inkling of what he meant.

Ed Schoonover left to bring the magazines back for me to examine, and I looked around the smoky, crowded saloon to see what Hap might be doing. The black-eyed girl sat on his lap, and Hap held his cigar so she could try to smoke it. She coughed, and Hap laughed, giving her a big hug. If Polly had walked in the door about then, I reckon Hap would have had a heart attack.

Ed dumped an armful of magazines on the table in front of

me. He bent over to put them in order and said, "You might as well settle down to do some reading." He stood up and shifted his weight, suddenly looking awkward. "If it hadn't been for those pictures of you in all these, I'd have thought they was talking about some other man. The funny thing is that this fellow, Lindstrom, writes like he knows you personal, although to my knowledge the two of you would barely recognize each other by sight." Then he said, "Until this last issue came out, I couldn't figure out what the hell that writer was doing, hanging around in Black Horse."

"You mean to say he's still here?" I asked in some surprise. Ed nodded to confirm what he had said, then he left me. With some reluctance I picked up the familiar-looking magazine. Over the drawing of the sun, with its rays spread up around it in a half circle, was the title of the *Chicago Weekly*, and under that was written, "A Journal of America's Westward Expansion."

The engraved pictures of "Tom English" varied. Some were based on the photograph taken in Texas, and I suppose the others depended on that to try for my likeness. A strange anger almost choked me as I began to read, and it must have shown. The men behind me moved to another table on the other side of the saloon. Whenever I looked up, people stared at me. As I read the stories, I could see why they would.

At last, sighing from the unaccustomed effort as much as from frustration, I came to the last copy of the magazine. But when I saw the title of its lead story, a pin prickle shivered up my skin, and I tasted the black bile of bitterness within my mouth. Without thinking I reached down and loosened Jason Field's old Colt in the smooth holster on my right side, and as I did, the noisy saloon jolted into silence. I looked up, surprised, then picked up the *Chicago Weekly* again. Gradually the clink of bottles on glasses and the scraping of chairs on the wood floor picked back up, together with the stifled excitement I heard in the lowered voices of dozens of strangers. I had skimmed the first nine articles, but read the tenth with care. I didn't skip a word.

THE COMING DEATH OF TOM ENGLISH
by George Lindstrom

[This is the concluding installment in our ten-part story. The complete series, with illustrations, will be published in book form under the title: *TOM ENGLISH, MASTER GUNFIGHTER.*]

How long can Tom English, the person we have with reason described as "the most dangerous man alive," continue to ignore the dangers which encircle him? He is now twenty-nine. Most men at this age have not reached their prime. But for one who lives by the sword—who will die by the sword—it is as though he is already as old as Methuselah, the patriarch who by God's own word lived 969 years (Gen. 5:27).

A revolver in the hand of an expert can be drawn and fired in less than one second. Tom English has faced this swift horror more than a score of times, and has lived daily with the ever-present possibility of explosive death. For a gunfighter life is measured in seconds. Each second of every minute, of every hour, he is at risk. How many seconds are there in a year? Tom English has followed this harrowing way of life for *twelve* years.

He has acted repeatedly as if he were, in some mystic way, immortal. He is not by any means the first to believe that he was protected by some "power." Many of our readers will recall the series I wrote for the *Chicago Weekly* on the infamous Indian war chief Roman Nose, who was killed eight short years ago. This is a case in point.

The imagination of our reading public had been caught by the hook-nose, six-foot, three-inch Cheyenne who bore among his own people the name of Bat. Already he is forgotten, but in 1867 and 1868 no Indian warrior was better known to the general public than the one Americans called Roman Nose. He wore what was for him a magic tribal headdress, made it is said by a medicine man named Ice. When he wore this trailing, feathered bonnet, he rode time after time through veritable hails of arrows and bullets—untouched, unscathed. He proved his invincibility by loping slowly, arrogantly, back and forth before his enemy, shaking his lance at them, daring them to do their worst. When he rejoined his wondering warriors, unharmed, they would be inspired by his audacity, and they would make their bloody assaults then with unparalleled ferocity.

Roman Nose had faith in the "medicine" which his war bonnet conferred upon him. However, he had been told that if he ever ate anything taken from a pot with an iron instrument the magic would be lost. A large body of warriors from the Cheyenne, Sioux, and Arapaho tribes gathered near the dry bed of the Arickaree River. They would on the morrow join in mortal combat with their common enemy: the hated white man.

Six hundred Indian braves prepared for battle. Roman Nose had learned that the night before a squaw in the Sioux tent where he had been the honored guest, not knowing of his taboo, had served him fried bread with an iron fork. The morning of the battle he refused at first to take part, but other chiefs prevailed upon him. He must go forth so as to inspire the braves, they said. Roman Nose replied simply, "I shall be killed today." Nonetheless he bravely put on his long feathered war bonnet, grasped his lance, and led the first attack. The Americans shot him from his saddle with their first volley, and that night he died.

The fact that a savage so believed in some form of heathen magic that he acted as though it truly existed is fascinating. We cannot truly believe that such a power can be. Or can it? Is it coincidence that after surviving hundreds of bullets and arrows, when the Cheyenne war chief stopped believing in his "medicine," he fell at the first shot fired at him?

The parallel between Roman Nose and Tom English is obvious. Both ignored great odds against them, ignored desperate physical dangers—as if they didn't exist. In the last article of this series on Tom English I wrote the chilling account of his facing three heavily armed enemies alone on the streets of Black Horse, Montana. The essential elements of this classic confrontation bear repeating.

One of these enemies held a double-barreled ten-gauge shotgun in his hands. I saw him cock both hammers. Another grasped a pistol already drawn from its scabbard. The third had his hand secured to the handle of his six-gun. Tom English, empty hands away from his sides, advanced deliberately against them. Sheer madness? Obviously. Perhaps now you can appreciate the comparison of him with the war chief, Roman Nose.

Witnesses of previous gunfights in which English figured had told me of his fearlessness. He was a legend before I ever set out upon my quest to find him. This time I stood not fifty feet away upon a raised sidewalk on the side of a hill, as though fate had ordained that I should be in a rough grandstand so as to view, like an ancient, privileged spectator, a bizarre modern re-creation of the blood-bathed Roman games. Unpainted boards rose up on both sides to form our primitive Colosseum.

Tom English faced the three armed men. Incredibly, he called out a challenge. And then *he killed them all.* It happened too quickly for me to see it, although it was directly before my eyes. I cannot, in journalistic honesty, describe precisely what took place, and I will not sink to speculation. All I can report is that I felt the shock waves as I heard the sharp reports of overlapping gunfire. I have pondered long about how I might describe the feeling that went beyond mere observation of that incredibly rapid concussive shock of gunfire. Then a silence fell like that within a distant, windless forest. I saw Tom English, a Colt revolver in each hand. At his feet three bleeding corpses lay in the street.

He has killed twenty-four men. Perhaps he believes, as Roman Nose did, that some "medicine" protects him. I would surmise that he thinks the twin six-shooters which he wears at all times provide this magic. But readers of history know one thing with absolute certainty: Magic never lasts. Even Merlin died.

I have spent the greater part of my life studying the lives of violent men in the American West. I have discovered none who has walked as closely to the brink of death for so long as Tom English. It does not require the gift of prophecy to know that this cannot continue. Simple common sense tells us that no mortal man may take grave chances over a great period of time without facing the grave itself. Tom English has taken such chances more than two dozen times. A gambler would give slim odds on his future prospects. I am a student of the man, and I say now that, given his own peculiar nature, he cannot survive.

With legions of enemies, and who knows how many foolish firebrands who yearn to shoot him down, lusting for the instant fame they would reap from such an act, it is safe to say that this publication will soon carry the obituary notice of the white warrior, Tom English.

Roman Nose wore his mystic feather bonnet made by Ice, the medicine man. Tom English wears twin talismans, made by *his* "medicine man," Samuel Colt. As the magic dies, so will the man.

I will remain in Montana so as to write the final chapter, which will be entitled "The Fulfillment of Prophecy." It will be the conclusion of my book, which will deal with the life and death of *TOM ENGLISH, MASTER GUN-FIGHTER.* The time is near.

I took a deep breath as I shoved the magazine to one side and reached for the whiskey bottle. I have gone to extremes to avoid trouble, even traveling all the way from Texas to Montana for that express purpose. The pain I felt in reading the foolish series of articles went beyond mere anger at the author. Few people actually know me well, and I guess they might argue in my favor, but things such as this, together with all the newspaper stories and the books from the past, would paint a picture of how I was. Falseness would be painted as truth, and for some reason the idea of how I would be remembered made me sick at heart.

I looked across the saloon. With the passage of time—and of whiskey down their throats—the people looked considerably relaxed. It seems that the more folks drink, the louder they think they have to talk. And if something is said that they think is funny, they have the idea that they are in a contest to see who can bray the loudest. When you think about it, being around mules—a subject that had caused me some irritation the day before—has its good side.

I walked over to the bar and Hap joined me. I've heard that after a certain age there are a number of more or less natural aches and pains that are common to mankind. Hap had wisely seen to it that he would on that day feel no pain. He weaved a bit and had to hold the bar to steady himself, then he told me how he'd been discussing with all the nice folks there our plans. How we were going to take all the cowboys to the East Ranch and finish up the barn and bunkhouse and corrals and get it over and done with once and for all. We'd been messing around with the problem too long, he said, pointing his finger at me. Our conversation was a little one-sided since Hap never stopped talking.

About that time I saw Thatcher and Emma at a table, and I

started to go over to say howdy when I saw a man sitting beside them raise his arm, signaling toward the bartender. As I approached, I recognized the man as George Lindstrom, apparently treating Thatcher and Emma to a drink. And probably asking questions about me. I knew that Thatcher was, in spite of his fancy hat and pretended knowledge, an ignorant country kid from Valentine, Texas. He wouldn't realize he was being manipulated. Well, what the hell, I decided, it didn't matter to me what Thatcher might say. I figured that George Lindstrom would be uncomfortable if burdened with too many facts. In all likelihood he'd prefer not to be restricted within the harsh confines of truth when he would have so much more leeway if he could give free rein to his imagination.

I turned away from Thatcher and walked toward a table at the back of the saloon away from the bar when I heard a voice behind me with a question in it.

"Mr. English?"

The hair on the back of my neck bristled as it does when danger nears, and I spun around. A young man wearing his hat pushed back on his head stood right before me, and his hand held a six-gun pulled halfway out of its scabbard. He stopped because the muzzle of my Colt .45 pointed right between his eyes, and at about sixteen inches away, it wasn't likely I'd miss. A hush fell upon the saloon.

The blood drained from his face, and he lost control of the muscles around his mouth. He looked as a man might if the buggy he was riding in slid off a thousand-foot cliff.

"Did you come here to kill me?" I asked.

"Don't shoot," he whispered. Saliva came out of his mouth, but he didn't notice it. He looked to be in his early twenties, and was ordinary in appearance: medium height, slight build, brown hair. He backed away from me, and I noticed that he limped. One leg was considerably shorter than the other.

We stood that way a moment, then I moved closer to him, and now the barrel of my six-gun almost touched his forehead. "If you had me in the fix I've got you in, would you shoot?"

"Don't," he murmured, terror distorting his face and eyes.

I thumbed back the hammer of the Colt. It ratcheted back with metallic noises, ending with a click. A nerve twitch would set it off, and he knew it. The gape-mouthed, silent crowd pulled back.

Speaking as softly as he had, I whispered, "If you held this gun on me, would I want to live or die?"

He began to cry, and said, "Don't hurt me."

The gun's cold steel touched his skin. "Answer my question."

"You'd want to live," he whimpered.

I pulled the Colt back, released the hammer slowly with the barrel pointed up, and then reholstered it. The boy's eyes fixed on mine. I asked him, "Are you going to draw on me?"

"No," he said, "I ain't going to do that."

"Are you *ever* going to try to kill me?"

"I'm putting up this gun," he said, still not able to stop the tears that streamed down his cheeks. "I thought I was dead," the boy stammered, wiping his face with his hands. Then he looked around. "All these people saw what happened," he said, looking sick. "They saw me beg." He looked at his hands. "I been *crying* in front of everybody."

"Most of them are too drunk to know what they saw," I said. "What's your name?"

"Most call me Gimp," he answered, making a slight face of distaste.

I took the young fellow by the arm and led him to the bar. Buffalo Ed Schoonover stood there looking bewildered.

"My friend and I would like two whiskies," I said in a loud voice. Ed stared hard at me and then the shadow of a smile crossed his face. He poured a strong drink in a glass for the boy and one for me.

Ed said to Gimp, so just the boy and I could hear, "He should have killed you, but now he's giving you back your self-respect. You're a mighty lucky kid."

Confused voices filled the saloon, and people continued to stare at us with perplexed expressions.

I raised my glass toward the young man called Gimp and said, "Here's to the future."

He gulped his whiskey down in one hot swallow.

I looked past him and saw George Lindstrom's eyes upon me. They glittered with excitement.

CHAPTER SIXTEEN

The late May sunlight felt warm on my back as I stood beside the wagon with its team of six big mules. Above me on the hill I saw Swede Larkins with his helper, Jingle Bob Doolittle, go into the new rock house which would be my home on the East Ranch. Swede and his helper were putting the finishing touches on the place while just about every man jack of the HC outfit struggled to complete the bunkhouse, barn, corrals, and pens.

Hap Cunningham sat in the wagon bed behind the two men on the driver's seat who waited impatiently for us to stop talking so they could leave. Hap spraddled out, trying to get comfortable on the hard, dusty boards. He said to me, "Within a week or so you'll finish up. Everything is almost done, but I'm sorry these old knees won't let me stay till the last."

He pulled his pants leg up and with an effort worked it over his left knee. The joint had swollen to twice its normal size, and he poked at it with his fingers. "If this pain was to go away all of a sudden during the night, I swear it would wake me up. It has been around so long it's like a contrary old friend that I've gotten used to."

Jeff Cunningham, his son, stood with me as the long freight wagon pulled away. They would drop Hap off at the HC Ranch on their way back to Black Horse. The teamsters had brought the last of the furniture, pots and pans, and such things that I had ordered. Quite a few wagons had made the trip as soon as the snow melted in the mountain passes. My plan had been to leave by now for Texas to get Sally and Rebecca, but the late thaw had slowed things. I had stayed with the men, though they could have worked without me, for I wanted Sally to be pleased when she arrived.

Jeff said, "I've seen Pa have trouble with his knees many a time, but he has never before been where he couldn't ride his horse."

"It was all that lifting and hauling when we built the barn," I said, referring to the way Hap had worked with the rest of us, alongside men thirty years younger than himself. By damn, he had enjoyed it, showing the boys he could still work them into the ground, but now he had to pay the piper for showing off. Just as Jeff had told him he would. Hap had snorted, "What in hell would a kid like you know about what my knees can stand?" When he hadn't been able to stay on his feet this morning, he had looked right sheepish, and had apologized to Jeff with a good-natured grin.

In the last month we'd had some excitement along with the work. First, the wild black stallion had again jumped the fence into the box canyon to join our thoroughbred brood mares, and this time we'd been able to trap him. We raised the height of the log barrier that sealed the canyon until it stood close to twelve feet high. It looked more like a stockade than a fence, and it did its job. The crazy, high-jumping stud ran at it more than once, but swirled away each time at the last moment.

The second thing that came along to cause us to get excited was when we ran across the herd of wild horses that the big black had left behind. A good many were fine HC mares that the stallion had cut out of Hap's remuda, and the others were stocky mustangs along with a few spotted Appaloosas that the Nez Percé Indians had bred in this country. Some of the Appaloosas had vertical stripes on their hooves, and all had strangely white-looking eyes. We headed them through the pass, and the long line of shaggy horses—they still had their winter coats—thundered ahead of us. By the time they reached the Basin division of the ranch they were worn to the bone and not much trouble to handle. We drove them at a walk for the last few miles until we reached the widespread pens and lots behind the corral. These had been built to hold cattle that needed doctoring and the like, and there was more than enough room.

The boys culled out the sorry mustangs we didn't want and turned them loose. But we kept around sixty good mares and maybe thirty colts in the lots. Old Chato Sanchez, the chuck wagon driver and general all-around handyman from the Lazy E in Texas, who was still useful around horses, stayed to work with them and to make sure they had plenty of hay and water. Laidlaw Utley also remained behind. He planned to start breaking some of the wild broncs to the saddle. I could tell that he was itching to begin with some of those spotted Appaloosas. "They got more freckles than me," Laidlaw said.

The rest of us returned to the East Ranch the next day, for we were in a fever to finish the construction work. On its completion Hap would supervise the big roundup, and the drive to the railhead with its loading pens in Bozeman with the steers we planned to ship to Chicago for sale. I would head out for Texas and Sally. It got so I could scarcely go to sleep at night I was so excited. I received batches of letters from Sally and Rebecca every now and then, and Lord knows I had scrawled enough of my own, but it's difficult to put down what you really feel on a piece of paper.

Ten days later Jeff and I rode ahead of the men, feeling proud —the way you do when you have handled a job the best way you can. We hadn't set a post or nailed a board that wasn't *exactly right.* We had fair worked our tails off, and we had earned the right to feel good. There's nothing wrong with real pride, for it's due you. The problem lies with false pride which has no merit to it.

"Jeff," I said, "I hope we can work together for many years to come. I've talked to your dad, and he and I decided it would be a good idea for you to spend next winter at my Lazy E Ranch in Texas, working with Scott Baker who runs things there. He is a good cowman, and can teach you a good bit." I added, "That is, if you want to do that."

I could tell that Jeff was so excited at the prospect that he could barely contain himself, but all he said was, "I'd like that, Tom." Jeff didn't go around wasting words. Come to think of it, with a ma like Polly and a pa like Hap, he didn't have much of a chance to talk a great deal. It wasn't easy to squeeze a word in edgewise when you're with those two. I knew that in a year or so the shyness would disappear as Jeff grew up. For some reason shyness in young people is especially appealing to me. If they seem too sure of themselves, it makes me wonder about them. Usually they're like Thatcher Stone, they are playacting. I laughed out loud.

"What's funny?" Jeff asked.

"Just thought about that crazy Thatcher Stone, for no good reason," I replied.

We came up a hill and in the clear blue sky I saw something out of place—something wrong: twisting strands of dark smoke rising straight up on this windless day. I felt a whipcrack of alarm and clapped my spurs into Lobo, my big-boned gray horse, and moved into a lope with Jeff riding at my shoulder. I heard the drumbeat of horses' hooves behind as the rest of our men set out in pursuit.

Dazed by horror, I sat in my saddle, looking at the unbelievable sight before me. Only the chimneys of Hap Cunningham's two-story house still stood. Smoke rose from the blackened timbers of the smoldering ruins.

Polly's bullet-riddled, bloody body lay crumpled next to a bush that sprouted fresh green leaves. Thelma's lay off to one side about a hundred yards away. Maybe she had tried to run. Both were naked. Both had been scalped. I didn't want to think about what else might have happened.

Jeff knelt on the ground and put the blanket from his bedroll over his mother. Then he knelt beside her, shoulders shaking, eyes squeezed tight.

Santiago covered Thelma with his yellow rain slicker while Stafford Darnell, her husband, stayed on his horse, looking to me as if he was struck dumb by anguish. I spurred Lobo over toward the barn. The gates to the empty lots and pens off to one side hung open. Laidlaw Utley lay stiffly on his back, his eyes bulging. Like the women, he was nude and scalped.

Then I saw Hap Cunningham. Scalped. Naked. Cut to ribbons. I felt a kick within my chest as my heart began to race. I had trouble breathing.

Both men had feathered arrows stuck in their stomachs and legs and arms at peculiar angles. They couldn't have been shot into them like that, I thought dully, it doesn't stand to reason.

Our horses were nickering and making low noises at each other, high-stepping around from the smell of so much blood. The ground lay red around the mutilated corpses, and the smell of death rose up to wrap like a muffler around our faces. Fighting back the sickness, I holstered the six-gun which I had drawn without realizing it. Somehow my mind seemed unable to function.

I saw movement in the trees on the hill above me, and slid out my rifle from its boot at the left front of my saddle. I levered a cartridge into the chamber, and sliding, cold-steel noises hung in my ears while I raised the Winchester to my shoulder, sighting on the form I saw moving slowly toward us. Then I lowered it.

Chato Sanchez stumbled from the trees, ashen-faced and trembling. Santiago had seen me with my rifle out, and he galloped up with his Colt held high. We stepped from our saddles and hurried to the old chuck wagon driver we had left to help Laidlaw Utley with the horses. Santiago and I helped Chato inside the shed next to the barn, where we found a bench where he could sit. While Chato caught his breath, I looked outside and saw the cowboys. They were carrying the bodies to the protection of the barn. Stafford Darnell and Jeff walked away by themselves as this happened.

Chato began speaking rapidly in Spanish to Santiago. I speak a little of the language, but I couldn't begin to understand what he was saying. At last Santiago turned to tell me what had taken place.

There were no Indians, I learned. Five heavily armed white men rode up, and Polly and Thelma came out from the house to greet them. Hap stood with his walking stick at the corral talking to Laidlaw Utley. Chato emerged from the barn where he had been pitchforking hay. The strangers dismounted and two of them grabbed the women. As Hap and Laidlaw ran to help, they were shot down. The outlaws hadn't seen Chato, and he slipped behind the barn—then ran into the trees on the hill beyond it.

Santiago said to me, "Chato saw them strip the people. Some were still alive when the outlaws scalped them. Two men walked over to Hap's and Laidlaw's bodies. They bent over and pushed arrows into them with their hands." His face twisted with revulsion. "They must have planned it all along, for they brought the arrows with them. They stole the horses—over a hundred of them counting the HC stock and the wild herd— and tried to make it look as though Indian renegades did the stealing and the killing."

Five men? We'd had them badly outnumbered. There were Hap's original four cowboys, the six we'd hired, plus Hap and Jeff. Then, Santiago and four Lazy E cowboys, and Chato Sanchez and myself added up to a total of nineteen men. It didn't make sense—unless they had learned that most of us were at the East Ranch.

I spoke to Hap's boy. "Will you be all right, Jeff?"

He didn't answer, though he stared right into my eyes.

"We are going to have to organize this thing, and do what has to be done. Get hold of yourself now. Will you do exactly as I tell you?"

Jeff nodded that he would without changing expression. But I sensed that he welcomed having someone take charge.

Miguel Flores drew me off to one side. Miguel came from Durango in Old Mexico and had the name of being a hard man. He had proved that to me in the past. He said, "I got the arrows

out, Tom. Had to cut most of them loose because of the barbs."
Electric stabs of anger bit within me, but I tried not to let it
show too much. "Thanks, Miguel," I finally managed.

The others gathered around us and I told all of them that Jeff
was my partner now, and he had as much say in what went on as
I did. Then I said he would remain on the ranch with the
foreman, Stafford Darnell, to guard the stock. I told them that
for now the headquarters for the combined HC ranches would
move to the East Ranch. There was no use having the men
living around a place where such hellish things had happened.
Then I gave instructions to the HC cowboys to dig four graves. I
pointed out a high location about half a mile away with small
trees on it as the place for the cemetery if that was all right with
Jeff and with Stafford. I said that to my mind such things should
be done and put behind us—instead of waiting for coffins and a
preacher. Jeff and Stafford nodded their assent, still not speaking out loud.

After the grim job of the burying, I said a few words. "Men,
these people lived good lives, and that is what we have to
remember. I've heard it said that you should count no man
happy until his death, but that is just not the way to look at
things. If a man or a woman lives with truth and honor, none of
that can be canceled by some awfulness at the end. Things that
are beautiful *can't* change into anything else, certainly not into
something ugly, no matter what bad things happen.

"Like most of you I was 'churched' as a youngster, and that
stays with you. It gives you something to hold on to when there
isn't anything else. I'll admit that the Methodists would probably have cause to denounce me from the pulpit for backsliding,
but the things I learned are no less important because of the
way I've lived."

I took a deep breath, wondering what I could say to make
things easier for Jeff and for Stafford, knowing that they probably weren't listening anyway. But the custom is to speak over
the dead, and it had fallen upon me to do it. I began again. "The
terrible way that Polly and Thelma and Hap and Laidlaw died is

in our minds. Some of you may have trouble in the years to come thinking about their happiness, their goodness, because of that. But let me take you back a long, long time. There was a man who had lived a very good life. A day came when his enemies stripped him and did awful things to him." All of the men looked at me attentively. "Then they hung him on a cross and crucified him. Yet the main thing we remember about that man from Nazareth is not the dreadful way he died but the goodness of his life. There just ain't no damn way at all that badness can cancel out goodness."

I pitched a handful of dirt down on the blanket-wrapped bodies, walking from one grave to the next to do it. "We'll put up crosses later; and we'll have a preacher come up here someday to hold a memorial service. He'll be able to say the things I should have said."

The men stayed behind to fill in the graves. Stafford watched them, but Jeff and I walked off down the hill about fifty yards away. And then his reserve crumbled at last. I saw the hot tears surge to his eyes. He gave way and lost control of himself completely, standing with bent head and shoulders while wave after wave of racking sobs shook him through and through.

The only thing I could think of was that I had to go, that I was wasting time. But I couldn't leave the boy. Finally he took my hand to shake it, then held it with both of his. He looked up to tell me I'd said something he would always remember. He held tight and said, "Thank you, Tom."

The time for words had ended. Santiago and his four Lazy E cowboys hurriedly grabbed what provisions they could lay their hands on, and we made sure we had our saddlebags loaded with extra cartridges. We were checking out our rifles and six-guns when Stafford and Jeff and several of the HC cowboys walked up to us.

"We're going with you," Stafford announced.

It took me a while to convince them that for all we knew this was the first of many raids on the ranch. We couldn't run the risk of throwing away all those years Hap spent building up his herd while all of us chased off after outlaws who, for all we knew, were part of a larger group that might be hunting *us*. I didn't really believe a word of this, but it convinced Stafford and the rest of them, and reluctantly they agreed to stay behind.

With relief I said I'd get word to them as soon as I could, and we made our preparations to leave. The fact was, none of the HC cowboys had ever been around guns fired in anger, and they would simply get in the way. On the other hand, Santiago and the four hands from Texas had ridden with me in the Concho River range war when we fought the Dawson and the Harris clans. I had spent many days and weeks working with them on gun handling, and had absolute confidence in their abilities.

Minutes later I swung up on Lobo, the big rough-gaited horse I'd saddled that morning. I'd have given a thousand dollars right then to be on Joe, for I'd trained him not to get wild when I shot from his back, but the outlaws had him, along with Ross, my big red roan stallion, and the rest of the horses. A fever mounted in me, an obsession for revenge. It didn't do to think about the fact that I'd never again sit in the warmth by the fire with Hap and Polly, never see Hap laughing with the crowd hanging on to his every word at Schoonover's saloon. But I couldn't help but think about all those things. I heard the echoes of Laidlaw Utley's cowboy tales, and I heard Thelma Darnell's laughter. And I saw them slaughtered and lying in their helplessness upon the killing ground.

An HC cowboy volunteered to ride to Black Horse to get the law, but all that meant was Jelly Biggs and young Thatcher Stone. I told the cowboy that we'd handle this ourselves—for it went beyond what law books hold. I spurred Lobo harder than I should and said, "This here is personal."

CHAPTER SEVENTEEN

We rode hard and fast. I had little doubt that the men responsible for the massacre belonged to the Bull Doggett gang. The world appeared through a hot haze of rage, and the only thing I could think about was vengeance.

Clouds built up behind us off to the northwest, and a cold wind began to make the juniper and pinyon pine branches snap. We kept our eyes to the ground, but it's not much trouble tracking over a hundred horses. I soon realized that the outlaws had too big of a head start for us to catch them before dark, so we slowed our pace. By late afternoon the tracks left the main trail that would have led us south to Black Horse. They moved west and crossed a shallow, ice-cold river, and headed directly at the almost vertical side of a wooded mountain. It appeared at first that we would be climbing the rock-strewn slopes, but then the beaten-down grass made it obvious where the herd had turned. We tracked them around a folding skirt of the mountain and saw above us where the ridge headed down, and another even larger peak soared up. We passed behind a knobby spur below the cloud-capped heights and entered upon a narrow passage. We had found the entryway to Bull Doggett's hideout.

Our horses slowed to a labored, climbing walk which lasted as long as the day's light. By now towering heights surrounded us on all sides so there really was no dusk. It went from afternoon to night in a very short time. Not wanting to feel our way along and maybe fall off a bluff, we pulled up and made a fireless camp.

To the best of my knowledge no one had ever had the nerve to follow the Doggett gang before. I had heard many people talk about them, and about the atrocities they were said to have committed. At the time I thought that they either did these things out of cold calculation, wanting to strike fear into the hearts of any would-be pursuers, or maybe the Doggett bunch had sick, depraved, and evil men who took some savage pleasure in torturing and killing. Regardless of their reasons, they had gone too far.

Perhaps they thought this time that the fear of Indians on the warpath would send such terror through our men that we'd pull back into some place we might be able to defend. But even so, if I were in their place, I'd leave guards posted. They might not really expect trouble, but they would be prepared to meet it if it came.

Long-rumbling thunder growled through the total darkness, and occasional flashes of lightning let us see, during these instants of almost daylight clarity, the wet black walls of rock that closed in on both sides of the twisting path. A cold mist began to fall, and we curled within the protection of our rough, wool blankets. I don't remember sleeping, though I guess I did at times, but before the break of dawn I rose, touched Santiago on the shoulder, and soon we all set out once again.

The acid of hatred that burned within me etched away all common sense. If it weren't for that, I'd have been more careful.

In the dull gray light before day we edged forward, and a sense of the hunt began in our blood. We threaded our way, occasionally riding around boulders as big as barns, and at one place I saw high up on the cliff side a little waterfall that dropped like a long white lacy ribbon, mist from it flaring over us. Then the trail widened, and I saw we were moving from a passageway bound in by cliffs into a narrow, wooded valley that opened up before us. The wind blew wetness across my face, and heavy dark clouds moved across the morning sky. They rolled and turned, making strange shapes.

The six of us rode abreast, almost stirrup to stirrup, when all hell broke loose. I saw Miguel Flores pitch headfirst off his horse

at the same time that a big-bored rifle's blast set off echoes of the
sharp report. His horse, terrified, ran wildly up the trail—head
turned to one side—trailing the dropped reins. Pepe Moya,
riding like an Indian, raced in pursuit. Somehow he caught the
reins and pulled Miguel's horse around until it followed him,
and then he circled in behind us.

We spurred forward into a leaping run, weaving past Douglas
fir trees and ponderosa pines, riding around and over bushes,
and a dozen shots rang out. A bullet whipped its whine right
past my ear, another hit a rock and split, screaming off in a
zigzag ricochet. Then Santiago's horse went down head over
heels. I reined up Lobo into a sliding, gravel-throwing stop, and
went back for him. Off to one side I saw another horse shot
down in a hard sprawl, the rider flying off and slamming into a
tree.

Thunder broke loose like deep cannon fire, and large drops
splattered off my hat as I tried to pull Santiago up behind me.
Lobo didn't like the idea of carrying double a damn bit, and he
danced sideways. I had hold of Santiago's left arm with my left,
and wondered why he didn't grab the back of the saddle with
his right hand as he trailed behind my spinning horse. A shriek-
ing bullet bored a hole between us as I hauled Santiago from the
ground with brute strength and awkwardness. He scrambled
his right leg up and over, then grabbed me around the waist
with his left arm, and we were off and running once again.

We pulled in our winded horses behind a stand of pine, and
got down as fast as we could. Shots from three directions splintered branches and cracked into tree trunks. Pepe Moya
crawled over to tell me that Sancho Fernandez was dead. Luis
Batalla had gone back for him only to find his neck was broken.
It must have been Sancho I'd seen, the cowboy whose falling
horse had thrown him into the tree. Pepe said that Miguel
Flores had been hit and that he was bleeding badly. The gunfire
began again and Pepe scrambled behind some trees.

I took stock and realized that, in addition to one man dead
and two hurt, we had lost several horses. Luis led our remaining

mounts to the back of the small mound on the valley's floor where we had taken cover.

Above us on the mountainsides at least three gunmen had us at their mercy. We were trapped.

The thunder crashed again and lightning flared. I saw Lobo rear straight up with a panic-stricken whinny, but Luis held tight to the reins. Somebody was groaning about ten feet away from me—off to my right. I couldn't see who it was.

Santiago's quiet face looked like a dead man's. I hadn't thought that he was hurt when his horse had been shot from under him, but something was clearly wrong. I propped his back to the rough trunk of a pine, and began to unbutton his shirt. "I'm fine, Tom," he protested.

I've seen many a man injured, but it's something you don't get accustomed to. Santiago's broken collarbone poked its ragged, red-stained whiteness through his bulged-out brown skin.

"There's nothing wrong with me," Santiago insisted. "Let me rest a minute and I'll be fine. Just got the wind knocked out a little."

I couldn't keep from thinking: if that ain't just like a cowboy to say a fool thing like that.

"You can't tell me that your collarbone normally sticks out of your skin that way, Santiago," I said, "so hush up about being all right. We got to figure out a way to get you to someone who can help." I wondered how in hell we were going to manage that.

I rolled from behind the big pine and dived for the trees off to the right. Shots kicked dirt and pine needles behind me, and cracked through the air nearby, making buzzing noises. Pepe Moya sat beside Miguel Flores. Pepe's hands shone red with blood clear up to his elbows; he had put his belt around Miguel's wounded leg. The bullet had gone in just above the knee, making a small hole, but leaving a huge torn-out place on the inside where it had exited. Probably the same bullet had dropped his horse. Somehow Luis had brought him to safety.

I realized the spot we were in. With Sancho dead, Miguel badly wounded, and Santiago hurt, only Luis Batalla and Pepe

Moya and I remained to face the outlaws. We had three horses for five men, and were trapped below skilled marksmen who held the high ground.

Just then the heavens opened up and rain came down as if a dam had broken—rain the likes of which I've never seen before. It rained pitchforks. A regular frog strangler of a rain. Within instants I couldn't see five feet in front of me.

"Quick," I yelled, "let's ride before this stops."

I thought I'd have to pistol-whip Santiago to make him listen to reason, even though he knew I was right. He reluctantly agreed to set out for Black Horse. Luis came up with the horses, but before we mounted, all of us huddled for a minute. "One way or the other I'll clear the guards off these mountains," I said to Pepe and Luis. "After you get Miguel and Santiago to a doctor, get Thatcher and Jelly Biggs and try to raise a posse."

"We'll be back," Pepe said with determination.

In about two minutes Luis was on his horse with Santiago behind him, and we'd shoved Miguel on behind Pepe. Miguel held tight to Pepe with his left, and clutched the tourniquet around his leg with his right hand.

I held the slippery, wet reins as Lobo tried to follow the other horses, and I strained to hear what one of them was saying as he tried to holler through the storm, but I couldn't make it out.

Three men on horseback rode slowly in single file, descending from the immensity of the rough mountainside. They leaned back in their saddles, holding their reins long as their horses picked their way with care down the steep incline. Chill rain fell steadily, but the force of the storm had passed.

I waited, staring through pine needles, not moving a muscle. The three riders were headed east of me toward the spot where Miguel's dead horse lay. My eyes moved from that point and focused on Sancho's broken form, lying face down, his head turned unnaturally to one side. He lay not fifty feet in front of the tree which hid me.

All three of the men who had guarded the pass wore yellow

slickers for protection against the rain. One of them followed
the others. He dismounted when he reached the valley's floor,
and stood readjusting his cinch, pulling it tighter. He made a
few loops to secure the leather strap, then turned to watch his
comrades. They rode forward cautiously, each with his rifle held
with both hands, until they reached the spot where Miguel's
dead horse lay. They circled the animal's body, looking in the
trees nearby for a fallen rider. Then they advanced again, riding
directly for my hiding place.

Still I didn't move. A ringing began within my ears, as though
a shotgun had gone off too close. I watched the two men on
horseback and I wondered about the third man. He didn't join
the others, but rather swung up on his thick-necked dun horse
and began to head out west. He passed the tree which concealed me with just a glance at Sancho as his horse trotted by.
Then he rode on about a hundred yards and pulled up, waiting.

The two outlaws walked their horses toward the tree where I
waited in the shadows. They still held their rifles high, and they
twisted in their saddles looking around—making sure they were
safe—when they reached Sancho's still form. One of them dismounted, still holding his weapon, and walked toward the body,
pointing his rifle at Sancho's back, just in case. He rolled the
body over with his boot, then shot him in the stomach.

I felt myself recoil, and felt a stabbing in my head. It couldn't
have hurt Sancho, but yet . . . I stared at the man who had
done this thing. He had a three-day growth of beard. He said
something and his companion on horseback laughed.

Yesterday's anguished hot rage had somehow vanished and
the terrible icy coldness which took its place gripped me. I
stood motionless behind the big pine's thick trunk. I looked to
my left and saw in the distance the third man waiting on a slight
rise, sitting where he could see the three downed horses and the
two dead men.

The gunman with the three-day beard now stood quite close
to me. He said clearly, "We ran all them sonsabitches out, H.L."

The man addressed as H.L. replied, "Bull should have been

here." He added with a flat-sounding laugh, "They didn't have a chance."

A picture of Polly's poor riddled body, naked and scalped, flashed through my mind. I stepped from behind the tree. "No," I said, "they didn't have a chance."

The men jerked as though lightning had hit them. The one on horseback—big, thick cords standing out from his neck—yanked his rifle around toward me. The bullet from my .45 blew him out of the saddle. His horse jumped sideways with a wild whinny and broke into a run, shying and kicking because the man's foot had caught in the stirrup and the body bounced under the animal's frantic hooves.

The man on foot froze, his eyes fixed on the muzzle of my six-gun which pointed right at his chest. Then he made a decision and brought his rifle barrel up. There are times when your mind works so fast that even swift movements seem as slow as if they're made underwater. The Colt bucked in my hand, punching him backward. He spun, both arms spread wide, and his rifle flew off into the air. Before his body had a chance to hit the ground, I shot him three more times. Wasted bullets. He was already dead.

I heard a quick clatter, and looked up to see the third man using his reins like a quirt, his horse in a dead run in flight down the valley away from me. Damn! He'd alert Bull Doggett and the rest of his men.

Behind the fleeing man surged the horse dragging the man whose foot had hung in the stirrup. Bucking and lunging the panicky animal tried to escape from its dreadful burden: the dark sack that repeatedly bounced from the ground and under its hooves.

Then they were gone and a weakness struck me. I shrugged it off; it must be the cold I told myself as I walked toward the grove of small trees about two hundred yards away where I had tied my horse.

I thought about how surprised the outlaws must have been when they saw me. They had been so damned cautious. Probably they'd seen movement when our men had retreated, but they hadn't taken anything for granted. After the storm passed, they waited with patience for any sign of human life in the valley. Finally they came down to make sure that the two men they had downed were actually dead. Then I had stepped from behind the big pine tree to face them, a six-shooter in each hand. I guess it had to jolt them, yet I could take no satisfaction from it.

When I reached my horse, I took down my bedroll. It seemed foolish to put my slicker on since I was already wet to the skin, but I figured it might help me warm up a little. When that didn't work, I hunted around and finally found some dead wood that wasn't too wet, and after trying for a spell, got a little fire going. I sat there, trying to warm my hands, and when I held them out over the small yellow flames, I saw how they trembled. "I must be getting old," I told myself. I had always been proud that, no matter how tough things got, I had complete control over my nerves. It made me feel a little superior to people whose nerves affected their bodies, people whose nerves controlled *them*. I clamped my hands shut to make them stop twitching and thought: Well, hell, it's the damned cold weather, that's all. Or maybe it's all this thinking.

Thinking too much causes nervousness. I don't like to consider myself to be a nervous person. When I lie down at night, I close my eyes and go to sleep. People who think too much get itchy and can't sleep at all. They lie there and get more and more awake. Thinking, I decided, is by and large greatly overrated.

Questions came to mind. Would Bull Doggett's men come after me, or would they wait for me to seek them out? When would Santiago and the Lazy E cowboys get to Black Horse, and when would it be possible for a posse to get through the pass to help? Should I hide somewhere and wait for the posse? I didn't really believe I'd come up with a solution to my problems. I've always had a lot more luck with questions than with answers.

After ten minutes by the fire the tenseness that built up served me with notice that I didn't have it in me to wait. I had to *do* something. I took out my six-guns and dried them carefully, and checked to make sure I'd reloaded them, which of course I had. Then I rose and stepped up in the saddle.

Lobo's rough trot jarred some sense into me. It's considerably better to be the hunter than the hunted, I thought to myself as I headed west, the direction the third rider had taken. I thought about him and the caution which had, in all likelihood, saved his life. "But the day's not over," I said to myself. "The hunt has just begun."

The valley widened until it must have been eight or ten miles across. I kept coming across blood on the ground left by the man the horse was dragging and it sickened me. It occurred to me that I might be riding into a trap, for the cautious outlaw ahead of me might well find a good place to bushwhack me. He had already proved that he knew how to do that. So I circled off well to the north of the trail his tracks left.

The wind bent the trees, and their branches threshed about, but the sky began to clear, and soon I felt the welcome rays of the sunlight. About then I saw a wisp of smoke near the south side of the valley.

Dismounting, I tied Lobo to a young tree, and climbed a tremendously tall pine that had branches sticking from its trunk almost like a ladder. I couldn't see for all the other trees, so I went higher. As I neared the top, the smaller limbs bent beneath my feet, and I took care to hold firm as I kept climbing. The wind's force pressed against the maze of green needles, and my weight seemed to aggravate the amount the treetop swayed from side to side. I looked down, and it almost took my breath away, watching the earth slide back and forth as it did. Forty feet below, old Lobo, who was a good-sized horse, looked to be a pony. Just then a limb cracked under one foot and I fell, snapping through young, fragile branches till I caught hold.

Your mind can jump off course at the damnedest times. It's

hard to say what triggers it. I felt a flash of excitement that made me glad to be alive. I remembered climbing a tall tree one windy afternoon when I couldn't have been much past ten, and I had the very same feelings now as I'd had then.

The sight of the Doggett hideout erased all thoughts except of the present. I saw a thin line of smoke turned sideways in the wind. It came from a sod house that had been dug into the ground. This kind of home, if you want to call it that, is not too uncommon. Lord knows I'd seen a lot of them in Kansas and other cold places, for they have the virtue of warmth in winter. As a rule, there is hardly room inside to stand upright, but enough of the lodging is above ground for a few windows which allow a little light to enter. They are built a thousand different ways, and the main idea is to get in out of the weather. I'm reasonably sure no architect ever drew up plans for one. The Doggett place had dirt and rock walls that only rose a few feet, and dirt and grass covered the roof. Smoke curled up from a chimney at one end of the crude dwelling. An old wagon, its tongue lying on the ground, sat off to one side before a log corral with eight or nine horses in it. Down the valley I saw hundreds of cattle and horses. No telling how many different brands might be carried by the rustled stock, I thought grimly.

A small barn had been built of new-sawn boards next to the log corral. They'd have bought the lumber in Black Horse, and with some difficulty transported it here in a number of wagon trips. The rustling business appeared to be prospering.

I saw movement then and made out two men leading horses from the corral. They went inside the barn for their gear, and then I saw them saddle up. A third man came from the sod house and untied the dun horse he'd hitched at a rail outside of it. He wore a yellow slicker in spite of the fact that the day had cleared. This had to be the careful man, the survivor of the three who had ambushed us that morning. The three men rode off, heading east back toward the place where the fights had been. I slid and scrambled roughly down the tree, breaking a few small branches as I did.

When they got back home, I'd be waiting for them. If I had a lick of sense, I'd hold off until help came, but as I'd told the cowboy at the HC Ranch, this thing had gotten personal.

CHAPTER EIGHTEEN

Lobo walked up to the Doggett gang's sod house, twisting his head over to the corral—ears tipped forward, nickering at the other horses. My every sense bristled—not just the hair on the back of my neck—telling me to get the hell out of there. Behind the barn I saw a narrow, grassy draw that curved toward a creek that lay below the house.

I stepped down beside the knock-kneed, weather-beaten wagon, and looped my reins through the wooden spokes of the left front wheel. Then, loosening my Colts in their holsters, I drew my Winchester from the saddle boot, levered in a cartridge, and stalked around the house and barn to the corral.

I saw no sign of any man. I examined the curious horses that threw their heads up to look over the top rail of the log fence. I heard some squealing and heard quick, dull thuds as a jug-headed sorrel mare laid her ears back and kicked a startled bay behind her. Then my heart surged, for I made out the two studs I'd ridden all the way from Texas. Joe and Ross appeared behind the others, standing tall and proud and a little aloof, the way stallions do. The rustlers had been quick to realize that in the stolen horses they had gotten away with were two real prizes.

I edged to the side of the house and looked through a window. No one moved within it. I had thought they might have a cook or some women, but I saw no sign of life within the place. Propping my rifle against the low dirt roof, I moved to the front and descended the hollowed-out trench that led down to the covered dugout. A kick from my boot knocked the door off its hinges and I jumped in, guns out. Nothing. The place lay empty except for a dank, sour smell. With relief I backed out of the low doorway, holstering my six-guns.

I felt it then. A hot, stinging flicker of pinpoint stabs prickled across my back like small, sharp fishhooks. I could feel their barbed tugging and I *knew* men's eyes were on me.

"*Don't move!*" a big voice bellered as I whirled, both Colts starting out.

"*Drop your guns,*" I heard behind me.

"Hands above your head," a third voice growled on my right, and then added, "Raise up them hands real slow. Real slow."

I stared into the huge bore of a single-shot Sharps buffalo gun. They take the biggest black powder cartridge made and have a killing range of over one thousand yards. The outlaw holding the Sharps stood some closer than that—maybe ten feet away.

Behind me on top of the sod house I spied the cautious rustler in the yellow slicker. He sighted down a Henry rifle barrel that lined up on my backbone.

On my right the fattest man I've seen in many a day held a single-action .44 pointed at my belly. He thumbed back the hammer on the "Peacemaker." To my eye he looked as though peace was not a subject he knew a great deal about.

"You ain't got a Chinaman's chance, you son of a bitch," the fat man rumbled at me. He moved up quickly, a lot faster than I'd have thought possible, and the long-barreled pistol made a blurred arc up and around, and it cracked against the side of my head.

I held myself on hands and knees, staring at the ground. A bronze church bell rang out its clamor inside my head and its clapper banged against the back of my eyeballs. Blood coursed from above my left ear down across my face and dripped down on the dirt. The kick that caught me in the ribs and flipped me to my back didn't even hurt.

Someone stripped my gun belt after untying the scabbard thongs on my legs, then two men dragged me to a tree. I heard voices through the terrible ringing.

"Throw a rope over that limb. Let's hang him."

"The hell with that. I'm going to cut his throat right now." A rough hand grabbed me by the hair and yanked my head back.

My eyes were clearing and I could make out the fat man, standing off to one side. His mouth looked crooked—like a poorly healed scar—like the puckered seam on an old dried-out moccasin.

"Not so quick, Henry, I'm running things here. Back off!" The fat man's words lashed out like a mule skinner's whip. The outlaw holding my head back raised the sharp cutting edge of his hunting knife against my Adam's apple. I pulled away as it razored a shallow cut just through the skin.

"Henry," the fat man snapped out his warning, "you'll do what I say."

The knife at my throat turned sideways, and the harmless cold steel flat of it slid slowly, in a vicious sawing motion, back and forth an instant across my neck. Then the man stepped back. His breath came out in rapid, harsh rasps as he stood there, staring at me with eyes that looked like dull black marbles. I've seen more decency in the eyes of snakes they have in jars of formaldehyde in some saloons.

The fat man stood beneath a long thick limb, unwiring the cut-off remains of a deer's shanks that had been butchered there. When he had thrown the bones to one side, he turned his bloodshot eyes on me.

"My name is Bull Doggett," he said. "Me and Henry," he nodded at the man who held the knife—who obviously still wanted to use it on me, "and Careful Ed been riding together for nigh on five years now. Along with H.L. and Buck."

He stopped speaking for a moment, then barked to the men he had identified as Henry and Ed, "Wire his hands up there where we skinned the deer."

Within minutes I hung from steel wires which cut into my wrists, and only my toes touched the ground.

Bull Doggett said without expression, "You killed H.L. and Buck, and I'm going to make you pay for it."

The man called Ed, still in his yellow slicker, stood before me and I was able to focus on the leathery, creased skin of his face. I had seen him somewhere before.

The men walked away, leaving me hanging from the two wires that looped over the tree's limb. They dug into my wrists, but I could tiptoe and keep them from breaking through the skin. The calves of my legs began to cramp and tremble, and I fought to think of other things to take my mind off the pain. Then I remembered where I'd seen the rustler who wore the yellow slicker.

I thought back to that April Fools' Day when Hap and I sat in Schoonover's saloon. A man left his poker game and sat beside me. He had thick black eyebrows, and a horny, beat-up-looking face. I recalled thinking at the time that it looked harder than a turtle's shell. That was the man called Careful Ed, the cautious bushwhacker who had stayed out of range when I'd shot the two men with him. That same man had once sat beside me at a table drinking whiskey while Hap spread the warmth of his happiness upon the cowboys and the girls who sat in a close circle around him. The strangeness of it struck me even now. "Careful Ed" had stirred up the men inside the saloon, telling them wild stories of terrible things that a pack of renegade Indians were doing. Folks out west have lived for many years trying to cover up their dreadful fear of redskins. The Doggett bunch clearly planned to use this fear as a way to draw attention from their own raids and thieving. Maybe people would blame the renegades, and set out to retaliate against the poor, starving heathen on their reservation up north of the Missouri River.

At least I had the answer to a question that had bothered me —how the outlaws had known so few of us would be at the headquarters ranch. Careful Ed had been in Schoonover's saloon when Hap told one and all we'd have most of our men working on the East Ranch for a while. Bull Doggett had acted on that information.

I gritted my teeth and tried not to think of the wires that pulled tight at my wrists. My legs were giving out, and with each moment the thin steel cut deeper. I hung there as helpless

as Daniel had been when they flung him into the lions' den.
Daniel got some outside help, but I saw none in sight. My total
vulnerability made me realize that circumstances can knock
the pride out of the strongest man. Fear crawled up my throat
and then sank back down and began to turn until it made a thick
spiral at the pit of my stomach. Fear is worse than pain. A lot
worse.

There was no way that I could escape. Santiago and the boys
would just be arriving in Black Horse around this time, so no
help would come for at least another twenty-four hours. I hated
to think what they might find when they arrived. Then I
thought of Sally and Rebecca and saw their faces clearly. I
hoped they never learned about the way I died. But then a
strange thing happened. As I thought of them, the fear got
pushed aside.

Splintered pain slivers cut circles in my wrists. The torment
dug deep furrows that seemed to reach clear through my bones
down to my aching shoulders. All my weight sagged, and blood
trickled down both arms. With my head thrown back I saw
through the tree's waving branches that the sky had completely
cleared. It was an incredibly beautiful day. By *God* I hated the
thought of dying. I kept thinking: there is still so much that I
want to do.

Maybe an hour later I saw the man named Henry riding up
the draw, leading the other two horses. He tied all three in front
of the barn. Then he joined the other two inside their dugout.
After an eternity, which probably was more like twenty minutes later, the three came out of the sod house. They were
sharing a brown whiskey bottle, each man wiping off the neck
before taking a drink. I couldn't blame them for that. I'd as soon
share a bottle with a victim of leprosy as one of them. From the
looks of things they were working themselves up to a fever
pitch. They stopped before me, and I straightened up the best
way I could, pushing down with my toes.

"Get a pick or something, Henry, and dig out under him,"

Bull Doggett ordered. "Then tie his feet so he won't be kicking around."

I fought back a rush of nausea as I wondered, *what is he going to do to me?*

The man named Henry went into the barn and came back with a long-handled shovel. He put his foot on the spade and pushed into the dry dirt. In a few minutes he had dug out a little pit beneath my feet. Then he fastened my boots together with a tie-string as though I were a calf he was getting ready to brand.

I hung over the shallow hole with all my weight held by what seemed to be red-hot wires. It took everything I had to keep from twisting up my face—for the pain passed belief—but I did it. And I stared right in their eyes.

"You don't look all that tough to me," Bull Doggett said, "in spite of the tales that Ed has told. He says you are supposed to be a famous gunfighter, and claims he saw you pull your six-shooter one day in Black Horse quicker than the eye could follow. But you can't put your faith in everything that Ed says, for he's widely known to be a wary kind of fellow. That's how come we call him 'Careful Ed.' "

The man named Henry laughed, but Ed retorted, "That's how come I'm still alive. I tell you, Bull, this here man is too dangerous to fool around with. You ain't never seen him in action, but I have. He cut down H.L. and Buck like he was swattin' flies. I say let's cut his throat and get it over with."

Doggett turned to him. "Now, Ed, you know people well. I've always said that. You told me this man was a fighter, and as such he'd come in after us. I listened to you, and he done just what you predicted. We walked back up the draw and trapped him without no trouble. You take pride in knowing people, like I say, Ed. And after riding with me for five years you know I'm going to make this bastard pay for killing Buck and H.L." Sweat beaded on his blubbery face as he added fiercely, "And he'll pay for coming after *me*. Then we'll haul what's left of him over to the trail to Black Horse and hang him from a tree as a warning.

He'll be the *last* man who will ever try to get the drop on Bull Doggett."

He waddled over to his horse and took a coiled rawhide bullwhip loose. He had it tied on the right front of his saddle where most men carry a rope.

Doggett lumbered back toward me and then stopped, feet apart, as he spun out the braided whip to its full length, flicking the lash at its end around with his wrist.

"I can snap the eyes out of a grizzly with this here bullwhip," he said. "I've worked with it since I was just a kid, and I've done some things with this whip that you don't want to think about. But right now, Mr. Tom English, I'm going to knock off your fingers. It ain't as if you'll ever hold a gun again. I just feel like doing this."

He cracked the whip in the air and it sounded like a pistol shot. The horses pulled back, jerking at the reins that tied them to the hitching post, although they stood a good fifty or sixty yards away.

The first blow hit my arm. Then he caught my right hand, my left hand, my right . . . I hissed my breath between my teeth, trying not to scream. I don't know what difference it might make, except the fact I didn't yell seemed to madden the huge, sodden maniac as he stood before me—heaving his wide, bull-like shoulders as he lashed out at me with all his strength. The shocking pain kicked my fear away and sheer rage racked through me. If only I could tear loose and get my hands upon him!

The whip whistled across my chest, snapped its lash through my shirt and around my side, spiking into my back, and it made me arch into a dangling curve. The cracking rawhide slit the air and whistled into my body and at times my face and neck. A dozen nightmares couldn't summon up the helpless horror that I felt. No words can fully paint the picture of the way nerves jump as muscles part beneath the sawcut tearing, beneath the biting, stinging lash of a bullwhip handled by a two-hundred-and fifty-pound man.

Two shuddering cones of pain spun in tight circles from both hands down into my brain, and when they got there, everything exploded into a yellow and red blossom, a convulsive spasm that passed beyond agony.

Water splashed over me. Bull Doggett spoke as though he stood at the bottom of a well, and I heard his hollow, echoing tones. "Wake up, you miserable son of a bitch. We're taking you down. Then we're going to strip you and cut a hole behind the tendons at your heels so we can tie the wires through there. We are going to hang you upside down from this tree; we'll string you up just exactly like we would a deer. Except we cut a deer's throat before we butcher him. You'll beg me to cut *your* throat before I'm through, but you ain't going to be that lucky. I want you to know what's happening. *I'm going to skin you alive* for killing my men. I'll gut you, and after that, you'll end up hanging like a side of beef from a tree near Black Horse. It'll serve warning to all men never to go up against Bull Doggett."

One man held on to me and with a grunt raised me up a little while another unwound the wires around each wrist. Then I fell on the ground, almost choking from the excruciating torment that pulsed from my flayed, bleeding hands and body.

The man called Henry untied my feet and grasped a boot to pull it off. Bull Doggett said he was going for his skinning knife, and through blurred eyes I saw him walk into the barn. Careful Ed walked over to the whiskey bottle sitting on the ground, picked it up, and tilted back his head as he took a long drink.

With a desperate effort I drove my bootheel hard into Henry's mouth. He spun down, hands to his face, clutching at the broken bones and teeth.

Somehow I found my torn hands around the handle of the long shovel, and I swung this back as I rose. Ed charged head down toward me. He saw me swinging the long-handled spade with all my weight behind it and he tried to stop, but before he could check himself, the heavy steel shovel cracked his skull as if it were a thick-shelled egg. The solid blow jarred me through and through, and the handle broke below the blade into a shivered point.

Doggett came out of the barn door as I rushed toward it. Looking at me with open-eyed amazement—as if I were the devil himself fresh from the pits of hell—Bull Doggett froze. He retreated, clawing for his pistol, then his feet tangled and he tumbled on his back. As he did, I fell upon him and drove the jagged, splintered handle that was my spear beneath his breastbone. When it stopped, I threw myself upon it, driving the oak shaft deeper.

Bull Doggett's eyes bulged out and his mouth opened very wide, as though he were going to scream. But instead of sound, an eruption of bright blood welled up in a torrent from his throat.

I picked up Doggett's pistol clumsily, for my fingers didn't seem to work. I held it with both hands and cocked it. The man named Henry took his fingers away from his red-streaked mouth and reached down for his gun. Then I shot him directly between the eyes. He fell and I shot him again.

CHAPTER NINETEEN

Thatcher Stone and Luis and Pepe rode slowly between the sod house and the barn, holding their reins tightly. Thatcher's rifle pointed straight up, its stock resting on his upper leg. Luis and Pepe each had a six-gun out. Then they yanked their horses to a stop as I staggered before them, emerging from the shadows within the barn into the late morning sunlight. I suppose I looked like the wreck of the Hesperus—covered with dried blood, with my clothes torn into ribboned tatters. They stared at me, speechless, and then looked around as half a dozen big black buzzards with obscene, leathery heads flapped their heavy, ragged wings and slowly fought their way to flight. The cowboys turned to see where the turkey buzzards had been. Clouds of flies made buzzing noises as they swarmed over the three stiff, grotesque bodies. The closest, Bull Doggett, lay on his back with an oak shaft protruding at an angle from his swollen upper stomach. His stubby legs lay wide open, and blood that had flooded from his open mouth made a blackish red puddle around his head.

"Holy Mother of God, have mercy upon us," Luis Batalla said in a stunned whisper.

"Madre Santísima," echoed Pepe softly. He twisted in his saddle as he examined Henry's corpse which stretched out awkwardly not far away. He lay face up, his jaw torn back, a bullet hole through his forehead and another in his chest.

The three riders dismounted and tied their horses. They walked past what remained of Doggett and Henry until they reached the body of the man called Careful Ed. He sprawled upon the ground near the tree with two dangling wires over a shallow pit. His skull had been cracked wide open, and they saw the dented shovel blade nearby with only a few inches of its splintered shaft extending from it. They looked again at the rest of the handle which rose from Doggett's inert form, and turned as one toward me.

I knew I needed to tell them what had happened, but somehow I couldn't bring myself to do it.

As though I weren't there, Thatcher said, *"What kind of man could do this?"* He asked the question out loud, but it seemed to me he didn't really know he was talking, that his thoughts simply formed into words. There really was nothing he could say to make sense out of the awful sight. The realization must have hit him that what he saw was *real* and not some terrible, momentary vision that would go away, that could be forgotten. Some things are never forgotten.

Thatcher, like most men faced with a condition that ought to make them speechless, felt he had to say something. There was no possible way to do justice to the situation, but he tried. "Jesus Christ in the mountains!" Thatcher exclaimed.

It is a peculiar thing that people often call out the Lord's name in vain when something astonishes or horrifies them. Or they use some expression better suited to a church than to everyday conversation. Even men do this who haven't been inside a church house since their mothers carried them in to be baptized. Perhaps, deep down, even such folks know that there are a good many things that go way beyond our understanding. Maybe cussin' is the only way they know to pray.

My head ached as though it would split from the lick Bull Doggett gave me with his pistol barrel. I must have touched it or something, for blood from the wound slipped warmly down the side of my face, and some got in my eyes. I rubbed at it. My head was light and for a moment the world seemed to reel.

"I hardly recognized you at first, Tom," Thatcher said. "What on earth happened?"

My throat was dry. I had to swallow before I could speak. Then I asked, "Where's the posse?"

Thatcher answered with a touch of pride, "We're it."

So many cuts lay open in my flesh that it wasn't easy for them to figure out what they should do to help me. The three men cleaned some of the crusted blood from my face, but they didn't want to touch all the bad places that lay open on my head and neck and body. My hands were almost useless, although I noted with relief that I could still move my fingers. They were terribly swollen and hot with fever, but it seemed no major veins or arteries were severed. Even so, most of the skin had been knocked off and probably some small bones broken. The wires had cut deep red bracelets to the bone around each wrist. Red and purple streaks stretched from these unnatural circles up my aching forearms.

I hate to go on about it, but I felt a good bit as if I'd been run over by a cavalry charge. I heard Luis suck in some air, and he said, "They tried to cut your throat!"

That little slice was so minor that I hadn't even thought about it. Each time my heart beat, it made a pulse of agony go throbbing up in an arc around my hands. That was what hurt the worst. The pain that radiated from them made it feel as though crochet needles had hooked their bent steel ends around the nerves inside, and whoever had ahold of the needles kept yanking on the nerves for more slack, with the plan in mind of making a bedspread.

Luis held a whiskey bottle to my mouth and I choked the fiery liquid down in thankful gulps. It somehow brought me to myself, and I remembered what had happened since the day before. I had slept inside the barn, waking frequently as the chills and fever struck me. After crawling around in the dark of the dusty barn, I had discovered some dry gunnysacks, and I rolled up in them for the rest of the night. I had still lain in them late the next morning when my three friends rode in.

"I don't know how much blood a man is supposed to have in

his veins," Thatcher said, "but it looks to me like most of yours is on the outside. How do you feel?"

I drank more whiskey, not wanting to talk, but I owed them an explanation about the sight before them. The whiskey made me feel stronger. I took hold of myself and began. I told them about waiting for the men guarding the pass to come down to check their kill. Hunters always do that. I told of the confrontation after they had fired into Sancho's body, and how I shot the two bushwhackers.

Then I explained about riding here, waiting for the men to leave, and coming in to find a place where I might have a chance against them on their return. I rushed through the rest, for I didn't like to think of it. I explained that Bull Doggett and his two men got the drop on me, then wired me to a tree. Luis and Pepe and Thatcher looked at the dangling, bloody wires as I spoke, and at the shallow pit dug beneath the place where my feet had hung. I told them of the bullwhip and how Bull Doggett told me he would knock my fingers off with it, and I saw Pepe wince.

When I reached the part where Bull Doggett went for his knife—when the three men planned to wire me upside down, naked, and then skin me alive—both Luis and Pepe looked as though they were actually sick at their stomachs. Both of them began swearing with earnest, heartfelt Spanish oaths that fair rolled off their tongues. Then, in as few words as possible, I told them how I had killed the men named Ed and Henry and Bull Doggett.

Thatcher hung on every word I said, his eyes bright. "That," Thatcher said intensely, "is the wildest goddamn story I ever heard." He looked at the bodies and said, "When that writer, George Lindstrom, hears about your gunning down the two bushwhackers at the pass, and then going bare-handed after three armed men—and killing *them* . . ."

"Thatcher," I said sharply, interrupting his fantasy, "he ain't going to hear about it from me."

"He'll likely write about how you rode alone into danger on a white horse to face the deadly Doggett gang," Thatcher said.

"We started out with six men," I said, "and the horse I rode was a rough-gaited, rawboned, old gray."

"It sounds better to say white," Thatcher retorted.

"I don't like to think about any of this, and I sure as hell am not going to talk about it," I said.

"It's too good a story not to come out, Tom," Thatcher said. Then he became silent, and I looked at him curiously, for he sat very still, staring off into the distance. I wondered if something might be bothering him, but decided he must be thinking about his girl, about Emma Lake.

Pepe and Luis told me that they had taken Miguel and Santiago to the doctor in Black Horse, and had been assured that they would be fine. Then they found Thatcher and went to the bar where a great many men listened to the story of the massacre at Hap Cunningham's ranch with growing indignation and a bloodthirsty demand for vengeance. But when asked to join in a posse to go after the dreaded Bull Doggett gang, they became less warlike. In fact they suddenly recalled pressing responsibilities that demanded their attention. Which led to the three men riding to my aid without additional help.

Speaking tersely, Luis told of finding Sancho's body, and covering it with brush to try to keep the buzzards and varmints off until they could return.

"We worried about the guards after we got through the pass," Pepe said, "but then we found two bodies with their guns, and more or less figured out what must have happened."

I don't know if it was the strain of reliving the stark occurrences of the day before, or if it was due to my loss of blood, but suddenly I felt very dizzy, my legs went limp, and I fell. The distorted, dark shapes of my friends rushed to me. A low, roaring noise filled my head, and my muscles twitched.

Luis worked over me. He tied strips from my shirt and from his into tight packs to stop the bleeding as best he could. My hands and wrists kept seeping, and before very long it looked as though I had put on a pair of glistening, scarlet mittens.

Then we set off. They saddled Joe for me since he had the smoothest gait of any of our horses. Thatcher saddled Ross. Pepe assured me that they'd be back with others to round up all our stock, and to get other rustled horses and cattle back to their owners.

Luis and Pepe hitched two mules to the wagon and tied their saddled horses behind it. They loaded Bull Doggett and Henry and Ed in the wagon. Ed, after all is said and done, hadn't been near careful enough. They planned to pick up the two bodies of the bushwhackers together with Sancho, and bring them all to Black Horse for burial. By leaving now we'd reach town before dark, they said. "It ain't that far," Thatcher assured me.

I sat on my horse, trying not to lose my balance. Someone had put a denim jacket on me, and it scraped across a raw place on my back. A burning swept across me, and I felt something that was close kin to a thrill, the uncomfortable inner trembling that fever sometimes causes. I looked down at my saddle horn, and hooked around it I saw the thick knot that Thatcher had tied in my two reins so I couldn't drop one or both of them from my bandaged hands. "I haven't ridden with my reins tied in a knot since I was four or five years old," I protested, but my lips were dry, and I didn't think that Thatcher heard me.

"Did you say something?" Thatcher asked, edging his horse up closer as we began to move out.

"I did, but now I forget what it was." He laughed. Then I said, "Thatcher, I thought I was a goner yesterday. They had me wired to that tree and I didn't have a chance. But they took their meanness too far. I reckon that's a trap that waits for really evil people. They always take one extra step that they shouldn't." I could tell he didn't really know what I meant.

"The wagon must be an hour behind us," Thatcher said as we reached the outskirts of Black Horse. He leaned over and took my reins just above the bridle's bit and stopped my horse. Then he stepped down.

He took my two six-guns from his saddlebags and walked over beside me. I looked at him curiously. He reached about me clumsily and buckled my gun belt around my waist.

"What in the Sam Hill are you *doing?*" I asked, completely mystified.

"The time has come, old son," Thatcher said.

Warning signs prickled at my neck, and an electric surge ran through me. It cleared my head, but I began to wonder if the blow I'd taken from Bull Doggett's pistol had addled my brain. I heard the stage-voice way he spoke, vaguely remembering the time when he had said "old son" when he faced Jodie Cade.

Thatcher remounted and leaned over to tug at Joe's bridle so as to get him started. Then we rode side by side down the main street. An open mud wagon pulled by four horses swayed and bumped past us. Dogs barked, and I heard town noises. It was a normal day. The sense of danger mounted, but I thought, dammit, this is too ordinary an afternoon for something bad to happen.

"I'm glad you never called me 'Buddy,'" Thatcher said distantly. "That would make it hard. My daddy used to call me that. So did my uncle."

"I don't understand a word of what you're saying, Thatcher."

He didn't appear to be listening to me. His gaze went over the curious men who stopped talking to each other, turning silently to watch us. As we slowed our pace, they lined the board sidewalks on both sides of the street.

I saw the writer, George Lindstrom, come out of Schoonover's saloon. He stood stiffly by a post out front, staring intently at us.

Thatcher said again, "It's time." He kicked free of his right stirrup, swung that leg up and over the saddle horn, and in one smooth, lithe movement jumped down to the left of his horse. A show-off dismount if I ever saw one. Ross jumped a little, then

Thatcher slapped his rump. The big red roan tossed his head around and moved off down the street.

Thatcher's eyes looked just as they had that day he shot the elk for no good reason, the day I'd seen a bloodlust in them. He stood not far from me. "You can stay on your horse, or you can get down and die on your feet. As far as those people are concerned, I'm the deputy sheriff and I've brought you in. You'll be shot for resisting arrest." He sounded breathless. In a hushed way he added, as though he could hardly believe it, *"I'll be the man who shot Tom English. I'll be famous."*

Thunderstruck by what was happening, I found myself standing on the street as Thatcher backed away from me. Joe, my horse, sidled away from us, the knotted reins still up around his neck. The crowd had grown until now they stood shoulder to shoulder. Their excited gestures and chattering stopped. They stood silently, waiting with tense and silent expectation.

"Thatcher," I said, still bewildered, "I don't understand. I thought we were friends—*good* friends." I began to talk to him, trying to break through the armor to find the carefree cowboy who must be inside. I guess I said disconnected things which made no real sense.

"You know," I said to Thatcher, "there was no good in Bull Doggett—I didn't expect anything from him but evil. But *you?* God damn it, boy, I know you—you're my friend. You're funny. Maybe that's the answer. Is this some kind of crazy joke? If it is, I've got to tell you that your sense of humor has sure as hell gone downhill. It has flat failed you." I saw it was no joke.

I kept trying. "I said before that I knew you. I guess I should have said that I *thought* I knew you. But I can say with certainty that there is goodness in you, Thatcher. I've seen it. You have such possibilities . . ." I stopped, for the look on his face showed me that the time for words had passed.

"Don't say anything else," he snapped. His face looked drawn —tiny white patches pinched tightly around his nose. He put his hand on his pistol butt. "We ain't going to talk no longer."

"I *care* for you, Thatcher. I've thought of you like you was family. . . . My God, boy, have you lost your mind?"

He didn't speak for a moment. Then he said in a quiet way, so the curious, crowding men nearby couldn't hear. "I rode from Valentine to Santa Rita planning to take you. But I was in the bar that night when you gunned down the man who tried to shoot you in the back. I knew right then that I wasn't ready yet. In fact the sight almost scared me off. But then you left town, and I trailed you—thinking I might be able to catch you off guard someplace or other. After a while I'd reach a town and people would always remember you. All I'd have to do was ask if a man with cold, steel-blue eyes had been there. They knew exactly who I was talking about. I learned you were headed for Black Horse, Montana, so I took a train and beat you there."

I interrupted him. "You had plenty of chances to shoot me out at the ranch or on the trail. Why did you wait until now?"

"Can't you understand, Tom," he said, sounding almost like his old self, "it has to be a face-to-face showdown in front of witnesses if I'm really to make my name—my place in history. I had almost given up on the idea until this chance came up. I began thinking about it out at the Doggett place."

"But dammit, Thatcher, you fought beside me—you shot Jodie Cade defending me."

"You were *my* man to kill, Tom. Couldn't let no other gun you down." A nerve twitched in his cheek. "No more of this."

He let go of his gun butt and bent his legs a little just as I had taught him. He flexed his fingers. *"Now,"* he hissed, his hand trembling in the air beside his Colt. Someone in the crowd cried out.

"You'll just have to wait, Thatcher," I said, bending over to tie the leather thongs of my left scabbard around my leg. My stiff fingers stuck through bloody rags around my hands, and it took me long, silent minutes to complete the knot.

Facing Thatcher, I sank to my left knee, with my upper right leg stretched out horizontally. I leaned my head down, ignoring him. I held the right scabbard clumsily with my left hand up in line with my upper leg. "You've seen my hands, Thatcher. Do you want to hang for murder?"

"I know about 'em. You do. But all those people are going to see is a gunfight. I don't care if you try to draw or not. I'll tell the writer, that George Lindstrom, that I was bringing you in, and that you wouldn't stand for it. In exchange for my full story, a book about the Montana Kid, he'll stand up as an eyewitness and testify—if it should come to that."

"Please, Thatcher, I don't want to fight you."

"Don't beg, Tom."

A crazy light shone in his eyes. He must have seen me raising the scabbard with my left hand as I propped on one knee and probed with the stiffened index finger of my right for the trigger.

Thatcher's Colt sprang up and flame flared out as it exploded a shot beside my ear.

The bottom of my scabbard blew apart as a slug tore through the leather. The heavy bullet bludgeoned into the center of Thatcher's chest and spun him violently over and onto his back. He hit hard—and lay there very still.

Screams and shrieks swelled all around me as a crowd of men surged forward, yelling hoarsely.

I made my way to Thatcher and knelt beside him.

"Why?" I asked. But he was silent. I backed away.

Thatcher's black hat with its chain of shiny gold Mexican coins around the crown lay off to one side upon the ground. An excited man, who must not have been looking where he walked, stepped squarely on it.

I heard a high-pitched, keening wail. Emma Lake, dressed in pale blue, fought frantically, twisting through the surrounding wall made by the crowd. She stopped above Thatcher, looking into the sightless stare that seemed to look through her. Then she slumped down in a blue-swirled heap beside him, both hands at her mouth. She reached them out and smoothed his hair back from his face. Tears rolled unnoticed down her cheeks.

"Honey?" she said hesitantly. Then she sobbed her question again. "Honey?"

CHAPTER TWENTY

"Honey?"

I jerked awake, my heart racing. Then I remembered where I was. Sally sank down on the couch beside me and buried her face on my shoulder.

"I'm sorry I startled you," she said, sitting up and looking perplexed by my reaction. "Were you asleep?"

"Reckon I must have dozed off," I answered. I'd not tell her about Emma Lake—huddled in tears—crying out that word over Thatcher Stone's body.

Even though three months had passed since my return, each time I awakened I felt a lurch of happiness at being *safe*—and in my own house at the Upper Ranch in Texas.

I had armed my men until they looked like an irregular company of the Mexican army, which is to say they might appear to be considerably disorganized, but in spite of that they were well equipped for war. I would by God *never* again be powerless in the face of my enemies.

The door to the side porch slammed, and a small twister wearing denim pants and a red gingham shirt whirled into the room.

"No spurs in the house, young lady," Sally commanded.

Falling backward on the floor as only kids can do, Rebecca shucked off the short-shanked, big-roweled spurs I had brought her from Montana, leaving them where they fell. She loved those spurs. I do believe she'd sleep with them on if Sally would permit it.

"Mama says we're going with you to Montana next year."

"That's right, Rebecca. She'll take your schoolbooks along and can teach you there as well as here. I hope we can start in April and come back in September before the winter sets in. You've never seen such snow."

"I'd *love* to see it," Rebecca protested. "Why don't we spend the winter there—please?" She dimpled her shy grin at me, and I could see what she'd look like in a few more years. She was going to drive the boys crazy.

"I'd like to get snowed in with you at that new rock house, the one you've talked about so much on the East Ranch," Sally said, with a grown-up version of the same smile. Then she said mysteriously, "Besides, there is a reason for us to leave for Montana a few months later." Before I could ask her what she was talking about, she gasped, "Oh—the bread," and ran full tilt out of the room.

Minutes later she swept back into the room saying, "I've got a surprise for you." In her hands she held a tray with a blue willow cup full of steaming coffee, and a loaf of fresh-baked bread. Kitchen odor memories from childhood curled within my mind. She had split the loaf down the top and at least a quarter pound of butter melted in it. "I'm going to fatten you up, Tom English. I'm sick and tired of people telling me you look as slender as a nineteen-year-old!"

Ben Jordan, who had been the marshal until age slowed him, and who served now as our sheriff in Santa Rita, sat in the rocker next to mine on the front porch at our ranch. The afternoon had turned an unnatural color that I have rarely seen. The day shaded into changing tones of yellow. It painted the trees and picket fence around our yard with saffron and with honey. Off to the west an orange haze of dust moved in—gusting before a wind that bent the tall, surrounding pecan trees, making their limbs whip and thresh as though caught up by convulsions. A golden light brightened about the house as sunrays found a window in the wind-whipped, rolling darkness that approached. Then the day turned to twilight as the sandstorm hit. We moved inside to the living room and closed all the doors and windows. Even so I knew the dust would soon coat every surface in the house.

"I read that new book on you called *The Master Gunfighter*," Ben Jordan said. "Like most of those we've seen before, it's poorly written and full of foolish observations. More than likely the writer, one George Lindstrom, didn't let the facts get in the way of a good story. Even when he told the truth, he couldn't keep from embroidering on it. For example, I was surprised to read that you're such a big man. As best I recall his words, you stand 'tall, strong, and invincible.' " His old, weathered face showed traces of a smile.

"Well, I am, Ben. I stand over five foot ten in my sock feet, and weigh at least a hundred and fifty-five pounds. Rebecca and even Sally look right small compared to me."

Ben ignored my comment. He continued, "I did learn for the first time some of the particulars about the massacre of Hap and Polly Cunningham and the others. Then Lindstrom printed a copy of the statement you gave to Sheriff Biggs in Black Horse about the trouble when you went after the Bull Doggett gang. For once he didn't add anything to it—he didn't have to.

"I talked to Luis and Pepe about it later," Ben Jordan said. His eyes narrowed as he examined me. "Them outlaws *had* you, Tom. I'll never know how on earth you got out of that scrape alive. You went after three armed men bare-handed—and you killed them all." He tugged at his mustache a minute, thinking.

Then he said, "At any rate, Lindstrom ended the book with his eyewitness account of the trained gunfighter who faced you on the main street of Black Horse. Your hands were useless—a good many men were there, and they could all see that only your fingers were sticking out of the bandages. Yet in some way you managed to get a shot off—and it took the gunman down." He leaned forward and put his hands on his knees. "You have pressed against the limits too many times, Tom. You should have been killed by all rights at least twice in Montana, but somehow you're alive. If you was a cat, I'd say you had spent eight of your nine lives. I don't want you to start believing any of that damn fool nonsense that Lindstrom wrote at the end of his book, the part where he said you were 'a man of destiny, a man who can't be killed.' "

I sat silently before his gaze. I had not discussed any of these events, even with Sally, although I had talked to her for hours about Thatcher. I recalled telling her—in spite of the things that had happened—how much she would have liked Thatcher Stone. People did. Emma Lake had loved him with all her heart, and even now I felt an empty place in my life because he was gone.

I don't know how much hell a man can live through and not go crazy. When I would wake up in the middle of the night in a cold sweat, I'd wonder if that was what was happening—I'd wonder if my sanity might have sailed off out the open window by my bed. One night Sally stirred, then saw me sitting up with my arms holding my raised knees. She rolled up beside me and took me in her arms as if I were a child. "Everything is all right," she whispered. I wanted to talk to her about the images that burned within my mind. But I couldn't.

At last I said, "When I was in Montana, I met an evil man. I feel funny using that word. Usually only preachers say it. I met a good man too," I said, thinking of Thatcher, and I spoke my thoughts of him out loud. "But he had a curious hunger for fame, and somehow he valued the high opinion of strangers more than he did anything—even more than honor, love, or friendship." We lay back down, close to one another, and I said, "I met a careful man."

Sally pressed the warmness of her face against mine and asked, "What in heaven's name are you talking about? Sounds to me like most of mankind would fit into one or another of those descriptions."

And I said, "Well, I guess you're right." I didn't say that the one thing that the evil man and the good man and the careful man had in common was that they all tried to kill me. But I killed them.

I folded Sally in my arms, and she said, "Let's go to sleep.

You'll feel better in the morning." She was right. When I got up, I decided, what the hell, the only thing that any of us can do is take our chances. If we simply go someplace and hide, we might as well be dead.

Ben Jordan broke in on my distant thoughts. "You have killed *thirty* men, Tom. That don't count old man Dawson who had a heart attack at the Three Points showdown long ago. And it don't count Mary Dawson who shot herself. You can't ever live again as you did before—I'm sure you realize that. You have to call a halt; you have to do something different."

I *hated* having to listen to him. My dreams troubled me every night. I should at least be free of nightmares when awake. I went to the sideboard and picked up a bottle of sour mash bourbon and brought it and two glasses back to the table between our chairs. The wind made the brass weather stripping in the upstairs windows howl like a bunch of tormented banshees, and the empty fireplace in the room echoed with hollow, fluttering noises.

"I can't talk of how my life has turned out, Ben. I just can't. My hands, thank God, have healed, and I've begun practicing again. I do this for hours every day, for it seems to be the only way that I can keep the bad dreams that I have at night from crawling over me in the day."

"You're telling me that it's too late for you to quit now? That so many are after you that you can't? Well, that just ain't so. Jason Field had a similar problem, as you well know, and *he* quit. I'll grant you that he didn't have near your reputation, but that part is a matter of degree." He yanked his chair around to face me. Ben Jordan said, "Now listen here, Tom. You've left these parts twice to get away from the hell your reputation has caused you. Both times you went from the frying pan into the fire. Now, this is what I want to say to you. I'm too old to ride thirty-two miles from town just for fun. I'm here for a purpose."

I sat looking at the old lawman who had been my friend for long years, hanging on his words. There comes a time when people yearn for direction.

"I've seen how you have armed your men, and that's the way it has to be. This is not a question of living this way until you think that matters have simmered down; it's how you'll have to plan things for the rest of your life. The robber barons in olden times rode with well-armed bands of followers. The Scottish chieftains did that too. Hell, Tom, you're probably richer than any of them could have thought of being, so that's the way you need to live from here on out."

"I plan to," I replied, "but in addition I'll wear and I'll practice with my Colts. I've never started a fight yet, and God knows I never will, but if it comes to it, I have to know that I can defend myself. I'll never be helpless again."

I had to break the tension, for though my body had almost healed, my nerves weren't as steady as I'd like. So I laughed and said, "It makes me feel right foolish to ride into town to visit with Max Hall or any of my friends, and have Lazy E cowboys surrounding me with crisscross cartridge belts, and guns sticking up everywhere." I grinned and added, "I hate making a fool out of myself, Ben, but I prefer it to being shot."

Ben Jordan wheezed out his cigarette cough and his shoulders heaved until the spasms passed. "You've got a lot of work to do, Tom, if you're going to keep all your Texas ranches; and if you are serious about building that big mountain spread in Montana in partnership with Hap Cunningham's boy."

"I *am* serious about all of that, Ben. And I'll follow your advice." I spoke slowly, trying to unravel the ideas that spurred me, the reasons why I felt I had to keep on building when I didn't really have to. "Making things happen, creating something that wasn't there before, is so exciting that I'm not going to let my pride get in the way of seeing it through. There is so damn much still to be done."

Hester Trace, green eyes glowing behind their fringe of long black lashes, came in from the storm. Her sun-streaked, pale blond hair hung down her back, tied loosely but efficiently behind her head. "You most certainly picked a wretched evening for a dinner party, Tom!" I smiled at what she said, and because her precise, British accent always amused me.

She turned to Ben Jordan. "Good evening, sheriff," she said as though he were the high sheriff of Nottingham or some such place. Then she pulled off her gloves before leaving us to look for Sally.

"If that Englishwoman don't beat the Dutch!" Ben said, admiring the slight woman who disappeared from the room. "She rode sidesaddle through a sandstorm like this one just to share a meal?"

"I guess things are lonely at her ranch since Roy got killed," I said, speaking of our neighbor, Roy Trace, Hester's former husband. "It has been a godsend for Sally to have a woman she can talk to every now and then, and the friendship has meant a lot to Hester too."

"That is an uncommonly lovely woman," Ben Jordan observed, pushing at his long white mustache. "If I'd known she was to be here, I'd have slicked up more." He chuckled. "However, I suppose sixty-seven is a little old to go courtin'."

Sunday's dawn brought rain. Astonished by the rare event, we stood close to the house under the roof of the front porch as sharp spray flickered at us.

Later, Hester and Ben sat over coffee in the dining room. It had been a long, lazy breakfast consisting of thick, rind-edged bacon slabs, biscuits, eggs, and coffee.

Sally and I excused ourselves. We went to the living room where we found Rebecca stretched out on her stomach on the hooked rug playing with the cat.

"Mary Jane had *five* puppies last week," Rebecca said. "And it won't be long before Ramona," she stroked the gray Persian's long fur, "has her kittens."

Sally began to laugh for no apparent reason. It was as if she were a child again, for she couldn't seem to stop. Her hilarity became contagious, and Rebecca and I laughed too without knowing why.

"I'm sorry," she gasped, wiping tears of laughter from her eyes. "Something just struck me that seemed funny, and I couldn't help myself." She rose and hurried from the room, and in a few minutes returned, once more in control of her emotions. She brought with her a pitcher and three glasses. With care she measured out a little apple cider for Rebecca and for herself, and a lot for me.

"We need to celebrate," she said, holding her glass aloft. "Here's to Ramona's kittens and to Mary Jane's puppies and to our new baby."

Rebecca squealed with delight while I asked, "What did you say?"

Sally had never looked prettier, and that is saying a great deal. And she had never looked as proud.

"But Doc Starret told us . . ." I began to protest.

Sally cut me off. "Doctors don't know *everything*. I've never felt better in all my life—or happier."

Rebecca caroled, "I'll bet it's a boy." Her deep dimples fell in place as she beamed. "Or maybe I'll have a baby sister. Son of a *bitch*."

"*Rebecca*," Sally said sharply, "I'll wash your mouth out with soap!" Then she told me that this is what came of the child hanging around cowboys all the time. But she was too excited to be mad.

Sally raised her glass again and proposed a toast.

"Here's to life," she said.

About the Author

H. B. Broome's great-grandfather was the U.S. marshal in that part of West Texas which is the setting for this book. The family ranch was located at Broome, Texas—named after the author's grandfather, the first man to serve as a director of the Texas and Southwestern Cattlemen's Association as well as the Texas Sheep and Goat Raisers Association. H. B. Broome now lives in Arlington, Texas.